"Why Argentina?" Was it easier to fight his demons in such an isolated place? Maybe working so hard with so few resources helped him cope.

"Before you ask, no, it's not about isolating myself from the world because I'm a recovering alcoholic and the temptations here might be less. They're not. And I don't consider this isolating myself from the world. My parents were humanitarian workers here for a while."

"I'd wondered if it might have something to do with your...shall we call it demon? But it's not, and—"

"No, it's not," he interrupted.

"Then I'm glad Argentina comes naturally to you. Choosing where you want to be because it's the right fit or because of emotional involvement makes your existence here easier. Oh, and just for the record, you overcame a problem, and I admire that. I hope it's not an issue for you, because it's not for me."

"You're the only one I've ever told, Shanna."

Dear Reader

Welcome back to Argentina! I love jungle settings, don't you? In this series, which started in Texas with THE NO. 1 DAD IN TEXAS, then travelled to Argentina in THE DOCTOR'S LOST-AND-FOUND HEART, I've decided to let Dr Ben Robinson stay in the country that captured his heart and fall in love. And fall in love is exactly what he does, in spite of fighting it every step of the way. But the heart always triumphs over the obstacles, and in Ben's case there are devastating obstacles.

Back in the day, when I was a young nurse and not yet the critical care nurse I turned out to be, I was assigned the one duty I always knew I didn't want: the burns unit. I'd been warned about the kind of suffering I would see there, and it was a given that the work would be difficult. I didn't fear hard work, but I didn't know if I'd have the heart to take care of the suffering I would encounter. But I was new, barely out of school, and couldn't refuse the assignment.

Yes, I did see suffering such as no one could anticipate. What I also saw, though, was the courage and spirit in my patients. In fact for my first few days on duty there my patients were the ones who helped me through, and I truly believe that was the first real lesson I ever had in the nature of human resilience.

My character Ben Robinson has suffered devastating burns in the past, and in REVEALING THE REAL DR ROBINSON you'll see some of the same resilience I saw in my patients. This story is about the true triumph of heart and soul in spite of overwhelming odds.

I'm on Facebook now, so please come visit me there at: http://www.facebook.com/DianneDrakeAuthor. Or check out my website at: www.DianneDrake.com. E-mails are appreciated, too: Dianne@DianneDrake.com

As always, wishing you health and happiness!

Dianne

REVEALING
THE REAL
DR ROBINSON

BY
DIANNE DRAKE

First published in Great Britain 2013
by Mills & Boon, an imprint of Harlequin (UK) Limited.
Large Print edition 2013
Harlequin (UK) Limited, Eton House,
18-24 Paradise Road, Richmond, Surrey TW9 1SR

© Dianne Despain 2013

ISBN: 978 0 263 23123 6

LP

Harlequin (UK) policy is to use papers that are
natural, renewable and recyclable products and
from wood grown in sustainable forests. The logging
and manufacturing process conform to the legal
environmental regulations of the country of origin.

Printed and bound in Great Britain
by CPI Antony Rowe, Chippenham, Wiltshire

Now that her children have left home, **Dianne Drake** is finally finding the time to do some of the things she adores—gardening, cooking, reading, shopping for antiques. Her absolute passion in life, however, is adopting abandoned and abused animals. Right now Dianne and her husband Joel have a little menagerie of three dogs and two cats, but that's always subject to change. A former symphony orchestra member, Dianne now attends the symphony as a spectator several times a month and, when time permits, takes in an occasional football, basketball or hockey game.

These books are also available in eBook format from www.millsandboon.co.uk

To Swede.
You were my first true inspiration.

CHAPTER ONE

BEN ROBINSON threw back the peeling wooden shutters, inviting in the crisp morning air. There'd been a dusting of snow in the valley overnight, for which he was glad. New powder on the ski slope, and one more day of skiing left before he returned home—it was perfect. Absolutely perfect.

In fact, everything about this holiday had been perfect. First time off in half a decade, first time in that half decade he'd almost relaxed. Tuscany in winter had been his dream, the one he hadn't expected to achieve given the way he lived his life. This was the best, though. He'd slept late every morning, then every night dined on his favorite indulgences—pastas and sauces and desserts—all of them sure to add an inch to his waistline. In between his indulgences, he'd explored the fairytale villages unchanged over the past two centuries, with all their little shelters for shepherds on the high pastures and the breathtaking succession of age-old churches, hermitages, castles and fortresses.

And he'd met Shanna. She'd shared some of that with him—the late-night dinners, the explorations. All very free and easy, but all very nice.

Ben's thoughts immediately turned to...well, whatever it was that had developed between them. Friendship? Brief acquaintance? Ships that passed in the night? Whatever it was, it was done. She'd had her plans for the day, he'd had his, and tomorrow he'd be gone. So there it was, come, gone, pleasant memories in its wake.

No, he hadn't had a holiday fling in the traditional sense. No kisses—not even a farewell kiss other than a peck on the cheek. No sleeping in late with her in bed next to him. Certainly no intimacies shared across the table during a late-night dinner. Then last night it had turned into a simple parting of the ways after a pleasant evening without any promises for his last day. Not even a mention of him leaving. But that was the way he'd framed it, wasn't it? Keep his distance. Enjoy the companionship, but not too much.

Play it safe.

Admittedly, for a moment or two, he'd wondered what might have happened between them if he'd let it. But he didn't even let that get past the wondering stage. No reason to because he would go home to Argentina *alone*. Continue his medical practice *alone*. Live his life *alone*.

And Shanna… A wistful sigh escaped him. He hoped she would come to the café this morning, the way she had every morning for the past two weeks. One last look would make his day seem a little better. But he wasn't counting on anything. He never did.

"Is that seat taken?" a familiar voice asked, twenty minutes later.

"Could be," he said, without looking up at her, for fear she'd read eagerness in his eyes. "If the right person asks politely."

"Who would she be?"

"Someone who would change her plans for the day. Ski with me now, shop tomorrow when I'm gone." Said in a matter-of-fact manner, taking great care not to sound hopeful or anxious.

Shanna Brooks. She was bundled up to the eyes with scarves, hat pulled down that almost covered her eyes and wisps of copper hair escaping their confinement, the way he'd come to count on. Breathtaking however she appeared. As she slid into the chair across from Ben, he couldn't help himself. He had to look across at her beautiful green eyes so full of life.

"That could be me," she said as the wraps came off her, layer by layer.

Had he really gotten up and walked to the table at the back of the café that first day she'd approached him? Pure insanity. But in his defense he'd stayed the next day and every day after that, feasting his eyes at the ritual of her revealing, the slow peeling away of scarves and hats and mittens. After all, he wasn't dead, just alone by choice, or design, or whatever the hell it was that had constructed his life to turn out the way it had. "But the question is, is it you?"

Frowning as she tossed her knit cap on the ledge of the picture window next to their table, she appeared to be thinking about her answer. "Did you ever consider that you could go shopping with me?" she finally asked. "Instead of me skiing with you?"

"No," he said, sounding too abrupt even to his ears. So he pulled back a little. "I'm on a mission. Twelve straight days of skiing without breaking a leg."

"What if your luck runs out and this is the day you come off the slopes with a tibia fracture?"

"Open?" Meaning bone protruding.

"Too much risk of infection," she said, tossing her mittens aside then starting to unzip her ski jacket. "I like to keep my fractures a little more straightforward. But I am thinking a tibial shaft fracture of some sort might be good." Something breaking between the knee and ankle. "Maybe a tibial plateau fracture?" Just below the knee. "Could be you accidentally hit one of those little mogul hills, popped up, crashed back down."

"No, I don't think so. Too much risk of late-onset arthritis with a plateau fracture. How about a tibial plafond fracture?" Closer to the ankle. "It has the same degree of seriousness, same lengthy recovery, but less of a risk for long-term disability."

She smiled brightly, then nodded. "Good idea. And I'll make sure I'm there after the surgery with all my bundles and packages, because I'm going shopping this morning."

"More scarves, hats and mittens?"

"A girl can't have too many."

"But knowing how I'm going to injure myself on the slopes this morning, would you actually choose mittens over my wounds?" This was dangerous territory. Too close to being flirty. He knew that. But after nearly two weeks he was still no closer to learning why she'd quit her medical practice than he'd been that first day when he'd shunned her at breakfast, only to find her seated next to him on the lift up the mountain.

"Mittens over wounds because I'm still on leave."

He faked an exasperated expression. "You created my injury, the least you could do is patch me up."

"Wrong specialty," she said.

"What was your specialty?" he asked. "Before you quit?" She hadn't told him. In fact, they'd been five or six days into their relationship before she'd let it slip she was a doctor. Odd thing was, she'd known he was. That had probably been the most he'd revealed about himself, yet she'd kept their similar backgrounds to herself.

"It wasn't bones," she said.

Her eyes turned distant. He could see it, see her shutting out whatever it was that seemed to be skimming the surface of her unhappiness. Or aversion. "Never cared much for bones, either. Not after I broke my big toe once."

"Skiing?" she asked, turning to face him but obviously not focused on the conversation.

"Ever heard of turf toe?" Where a person pro-
pelled themselves forward by pushing off on the
big toe, resulting in their weight shifting to their
other foot. If the toe stayed flat on the ground
and didn't lift to push off, the joint injury, associated with athletes who played on artificial turf,
resulted.

That caught her interest for real. "You played
soccer? Or football?"

"No. I was chasing an angora goat."

Her eyes widened. "Not sure I want to ask why."

He chuckled. "Nothing…untoward. My parents
raised goats and sheep for the wool. The one I was
shearing got away."

"Hence turf toe. But that's a ligament strain,
not a break."

"Or in my case both."

Laughing, Shanna said, "Poor Ben. He doesn't
even get the glory of claiming some great ath-
letic accident. You don't really tell many people
you had a goat injury, do you? Very embarrass-
ing, Ben. *Very.*"

"So would someone pointing out how embar-
rassing my embarrassment was." He flagged over
the server, who immediately brought cups of coffee to the table.

"I don't suppose I could coax you into a send-off mimosa this morning, could I?" she asked. "Since this is our last morning together."

"Coffee's good," he said. Revealing a goat injury was enough for one day. No need to reveal any more than that.

"Champagne and orange juice is better." She paused, thought for a moment. A knowing expression tracked across her face in delayed measures as the full awareness of what she'd just realized finally struck her. "But you don't drink at all, do you? Not a drop."

"How do you figure?"

"When we've had dinner I've had wine a few times, yet you've always ordered..." She shrugged. "You're right. Coffee's good. And you should have told me, Ben. I wouldn't have..." Shaking her head, she picked up her coffee mug and held on to it for dear life. "I know we're not involved, but you should have told me."

"There's nothing to tell." Such a huge lie. But why say anything and ruin a little light flirting, a few pleasant meals, a couple runs down the slope? There was nothing sloppy, nothing sentimental about the two of them and he'd appreciated that because it had been a step totally outside his normal self. Now, though, it was time to step back in, and inside Ben Robinson there was no need to tell anybody anything about himself. Those who knew knew. Those who didn't never would.

"Nothing except a drinking problem? In the past, I'm assuming. It would have been nice to know, because I wouldn't have had wine—"

"Wouldn't have had wine?" he interrupted. "What people do or don't do around me doesn't bother me. I'm not influenced."

"Maybe you're not influenced, but I don't like being insensitive. If you'd told me..."

"It would have changed things between us. You would have been a little more on guard. Or wondered what caused me to turn into an alcoholic, which I am, by the way. That wasn't the kind of relationship we were having." And now started the awkwardness between them, when all they should have been doing was having a carefree last day. It was another perfect example of why he didn't get involved. She'd peeled back one of his layers and discovered the first well-guarded aspect of a man called Ben Robinson. Yeah, he was an alcoholic. Yeah, he did still struggle with the temptation occasionally, even though he hadn't taken a drink in a decade. Yeah, it was a social barrier.

"Or it would have been a reference in passing. Not everybody is harsh in their judgments, Ben. Trust me, I understand how moments of weakness can escalate. But you're right. We didn't establish the kind of relationship where confessions were required. Anyway, I've enjoyed our connection for what it was—a few hours of fun with a man who speaks my language. It made my sabbatical easier." She reached across and squeezed his hand. "Although I *am* sorry you struggled with alcohol, Ben. Glad you made it through, but sorry for whatever took you on that journey." She fixed her gaze on the view of the mountain as she let go of his hand.

Then breakfast came, they ate, made light conversation about insignificant things, endured more silence between them than they had before. And it was over. Done. They descended into that so-called mutual parting of the ways of infamous fame and he went to ski while she went to shop. Afterward Ben Robinson, forever alone as he'd pledged himself to be, spent the thirty-six hours that came in a plane or between flights wondering why the hell he hadn't just lived in the moment for once. Or lived *for* the moment.

"Because reality returns after the moment," he

muttered to himself, fastening his seat belt as he prepared for the last stretch of his journey home. Fourteen hours in the air left him with a lot of time to think, a lot of time to regret.

"Coffee, tea, soft drink? Glass of wine?" the flight attendant asked him as he tried stretching out his lanky legs in too tight a space. "Or a cocktail, sir? We have all the standards— gin, vodka, Scotch..."

Glancing at the beverage cart, he saw the array of small booze bottles, all ready for pouring. Except he didn't drink anymore. That was what he'd told Shanna, and that was the way he'd lived his life for a long, long time now.

Even so, nights like this weakened his resolve. Made it tougher on him to fight when he wasn't sure what he was fighting more—the booze, or himself.

Then he thought about Shanna's green eyes, and the way she'd looked at him that first morning when all she'd really wanted was the view of the mountain he had. He'd seen vitality, a spark that had made him change his ways for the duration of his holiday. He'd opened the door just a crack to let somebody in. Only now the holiday was over and Shanna was but a memory. And like every other time he'd been tempted to break his resolve, he'd take a deep breath and remind himself about his responsibilities. Then stay on track. "Water, please," he told the attendant. "Water will be fine."

"Okay, Ben Robinson, just who are you?" Two days ago he'd left her sitting in the café, wondering what it was about her that clearly hadn't inspired his trust. And it wasn't just about his drinking. It was about everything. They'd spent some nice time together, but every minute of it had shown her how obviously distant he was. More than that, how distant he wanted to stay. Being alone together—that was how she'd felt when she'd been with him. Alone. They'd shared a ski lift, shared meals, shared a few walks, shared time. What he hadn't shared had been himself.

"So who are you, really?" she asked her computer screen as she typed his name into a search engine. "And why are you in Argentina?" The even bigger question was, *Where in Argentina?* Because it was only after he'd gone that she'd realized she didn't know. Realized she didn't even have his phone number. Realized he had merely been a stranger passing through, stopping for a few moments without making a connection.

Except he had. She wasn't sure what kind it was, but here she was, looking for information about him, wondering what it was about Ben Robinson that pulled her in.

Maybe it was a simple thing, really. He was so found, and she was so lost. *Found* had a certain sense of stability to it. A security she'd thought she had but had then discovered it had all been an illusion. Ben didn't give in to illusions. Didn't even let them come near. Sure, it was a harsh way to live your life, but there was safety in that harshness, and that was what she needed—that safety. Because the rug had been pulled out from under her. All those things she'd defined her life by— gone now. One tug and she was flailing.

But Ben had flailed, hadn't he? The scars on his neck accounted for some kind of flailing. So did the alcohol. He'd recovered, though, and that was what eluded her. How to recover. How to even start. Or where to start. Which was why she was keying in his name and connecting it to Argentina medical facilities.

Her life was open now. She had no place to be and nothing to do until she figured out how to be someone else. A journey to start over—that was essentially what she was about. And Ben knew that journey. It was, in a word, *dispassion.* It's where he lived, where he succeeded. It's where she needed to live and succeed if she were to continue in medicine. Because if she couldn't find that place in her own soul, what she loved would destroy her. So her choices were two: learn how to separate herself completely from her passion; or walk away from it altogether.

That was why Ben fascinated her. He'd separated himself. She'd seen that the first morning he'd refused to sit across the table from her, then later sitting shoulder to shoulder on a ski lift with her in near silence. Yet he was a doctor. Owned a little hospital. It didn't seem to jibe. Or maybe it did. Maybe Ben was the master of that separation she needed to find, and embrace.

"I'm probably crazy, Ben," she said to the screen as a series of links popped up, none of them leading her to her object of fascination. "But I don't think we're through. If I can find you…" she said to the next futile attempt. The one after that she cursed, and the one after that she merely grunted at. But the next attempt…maybe not so futile. "Are you my Ben Robinson?" she asked the figure who finally popped up on her screen. Handsome, not a particularly friendly smile on his face. Same eyes, only hidden behind glasses. Shorter hair, no three-day growth of beard covering his face.

"Dr. Benjamin Robinson, owner and director of…" Shanna breathed a sigh of relief. No, she wasn't crazy. She was simply looking for a way home and Ben was the map. So, with that in mind, Dr. Shanna Brooks booked a plane ticket, packed her bags and headed to Argentina.

"Are you finally back in the swing of things?" Dr. Amanda Kenner asked her brother. "Or do you need some holiday recovery time?"

"Another week or two in Tuscany would work. But if I can't have that then, yes, I'm back in the swing of things." He gestured for her to follow him through the central ward in the forty-patient-capacity hospital called Caridad. There were no epidemics now, thanks to Amanda's husband, who'd solved a recent crisis with giardiasis. But there were still patients to be seen, and he was glad to be back on steady ground. This was where he belonged, and as much as he'd loved Tuscany, waiting another half decade for his next holiday would suit him fine. Getting away was good, but this is where he belonged.

Although…his thoughts drifted back to Shanna. Thoughts filled with regrets and missed opportunities. He was a normal man in those things, had desires, hopes and dreams. But he also had his reality, the one that told him who he was every time he looked into a mirror. And that was the fact of his life that never changed.

"You couldn't stand being away any longer," Amanda teased. "In fact, I'm surprised you stayed as long as you did."

"It was a nice place. Good food, the best skiing I've ever done. And Signora Palmadessa ran an outstanding little inn. But it was a holiday, and we can't spend our lives on holiday, can we?"

"Am I hearing some sadness in your voice?" Amanda asked.

He shook his head. "Exhaustion. It was a long trip home." Emotionally and physically.

Before they walked through the doors of the ward, Amanda stopped in front of her brother and studied his face for a moment. "You met someone there, didn't you?"

He nodded. "Not like you think, though."

"But you fell in love with her. You had a holiday fling and fell in love."

"No fling, no falling in love. She was just a nice way to pass some pleasant hours. Someone to take the stigma off eating alone. No big deal, really."

"Then why the wistful sigh?"

"Not wistful. Agitated. I have patients to see and you're standing in my way."

"I'm sorry it didn't work out, Ben. Whatever it was between you, whoever she was, I'm sorry it didn't work out, because I was truly hoping you'd meet a beautiful Tuscan woman who'd steal your heart at first sight, then you'd have some kind of wild adventure with her. Maybe even get married and send me an email telling me you were staying there to have a full life and lots of babies."

She backed away from Ben and brushed tears from her eyes. "Anything that makes you happy… that's all I want. All I've ever wanted for you."

"I know and I appreciate it. But I'm reconciled to what I have, what I am, Amanda," he said gently. "It's taken me a lot of years to come to terms with it, but it's a decent choice, all things considered. So now it's your turn to comes to terms with it. Okay?" Being alone *had* been his choice since he'd been fifteen. More strongly confirmed at age twenty-two with a fiancée, Nancy Collier, who'd gasped, but not in ecstasy, the first time they'd made love. Or attempted to.

The look on her face then the apologies and the discomfort...no man wanted to face that. But what he'd faced that day, even more than Nancy's repulsion over his physical scars, had been the fact that this was the way it was always going to be. One look at the monster, and people turned away. And that was what unleashed the real monster.

Now it was easier to not let them look.

"No, it's not okay. Your choice is too hard, Ben. You're too hard on yourself, and it worries me, because if someone wonderful did come along..."

Someone wonderful, like Shanna... "It is what it is. My life is good, I'm not alone." Subconsciously, he brushed his fingers across the scars on his neck. "And you're too sentimental right now. Pregnancy hormones running amuck with your emotions, or something like that. How's my nephew, by the way?" he asked, fervently hoping to get off the circumstances of his life, for which there was no solution. "I've missed him. Wondered how he was settling into family life." He was referring to Ezequiel, the twelve-year-old Amanda and Jack had recently adopted. Also the sure proof there were happy endings out there. Just not for him.

"He and Jack are out on a medical run, but they should be back in a couple of days. Jack decided it's good to take Ezequiel with him whenever he can when he goes out on short trips. It gives them some quality father-son time, and also gives Ezequiel a sense of purpose, pretending to be a doctor's assistant." She smiled with pride. "My new son is like a sponge. He absorbs everything, and he's so anxious to learn and experience new things. I think he might be a doctor someday."

"Children have so many expectations at that age," Ben commented as he stepped around Amanda and pulled open the door to the women's ward. He'd had those same expectations once. Not about being a doctor so much as the other things life might hold in store for him. In his youthful naivety he had just been waiting for the world to open up for him so he could take whatever he wanted.

Then one day it had ended. *Everything.* No more expectations, no more youthful hopes and dreams because those didn't happen where he'd spent the next year of his life—in a burns ward, fighting for his life, going through skin graft after skin graft, battling any number of opportunistic infections trying to kill him by various degrees.

Those had been the days when his expectations had turned away from the world and centered only on surviving through the next few minutes, the next hour, the next day.

"I'm sorry it didn't work out," she said as they walked shoulder to shoulder to their first patient. "Your affair in Tuscany. I'm sorry it didn't work out."

"There was nothing to work out," he said, stopping short of the bed where his first patient was dozing, then turned to face his sister. "See, that's the thing. She wasn't into me. If she had been, I wouldn't have spent those few days with her. That's the way it is, Amanda, and it's not going to change." He gave her a squeeze on the arm. "I love you for trying, but you've more important things to worry about now. And in the meantime I've got a middle-aged woman, bad diet, uncontrolled diabetes to look after."

"Do you remember that treehouse Dad built us?" Amanda asked.

"The one where I wouldn't let girls inside?" he replied, wondering where this was going.

"But I always managed to get in, Ben."

"And left dolls there."

"I knew you didn't want a sister, knew you felt threatened when Mom and Dad adopted me. I was only five, but I could see it in you. See the resentment and the fear that maybe they were replacing you with me. It shows, Ben. It always shows on you."

"But we eventually had fun there when I finally managed to get rid of the dolls."

"And the pink curtains Mother made for the treehouse."

Good memories, those days when his family had been happy. They were good to hold on to, especially when the darker days had prevailed. "So, are you thinking we should build a treehouse for Ezequiel? Is that where this conversation is leading?"

"You know it's not," she whispered, fighting back tears. "In the days before you accepted me as your sister, you hid in that treehouse. Refused to come out. I watched from my bedroom window. Could see you in there angry, hurt…crying. Ben, you have to come out of the treehouse. You can't spend your whole life hiding."

"I run a hospital. I work twenty hours a day, seven days a week. That's not hiding."

"There are different ways to hide, Ben." She swiped at her tears. "Anyway, you've got patients to see, I've got patients to see…"

"I'm fine, Amanda," he said as she walked away. She didn't answer, though. Just kept on walking. And he…well, he just tried to blot it out of his mind. What else was there?

"So, I didn't expect to see you back here so soon," he said, turning his attention to his patient as he pulled up a chair next to the bed, and sat down. "It's only been three weeks, Maria, which means we need to talk again about the things that can happen to you if you don't take better care of yourself." Said to a lady who was eyeing a plate of pastries next to her bed, left there by a too-sympathetic husband.

Sighing, Ben began the spiel he'd used on her ten times before. Apparently to no avail again. But he understood. It was never easy giving up what you loved, or what you wanted, no matter what the reason. Sometimes, though, life was just plain cruel and forced it on you. "First, you could have heart complications…" Something he assiduously avoided in his personal life.

CHAPTER TWO

"THAT way," the disagreeable driver grunted. The filter of his cigarette was stuck between his lips, just hanging there, no more cigarette left to smoke. "I don't go there."

"I'm not surprised," she quipped, tossing her oversized duffel on the ground outside the taxi, not expecting the driver to help her. Which he didn't. But he was quick to extend his meaty hand out the window for a tip. The only tip she wanted to give him was to quit smoking and adopt a better disposition, but handing him a few pesos was easier. So she handed him a fist full of notes, then watched as he counted his money, grunted, then drove off without a care or concern over how she was going to accomplish the next leg of her journey.

For all she knew, she was nowhere near the village, called *Aldea de Cascada*—village by the waterfall—which she'd been told was also called *Aldea de Hospital,* thanks to Ben's hospital.

Major disillusion certainly caused major life changes. And the gnats swarming her, either to glom onto the carbon dioxide was she exhaling or the sweat she was sweating like she'd never sweated before, were sure testament to that.

"Okay," she said, picking up the duffel and slinging it over her shoulder, which threw her off balance and sent her tumbling backward a couple of steps. "Just do it. You want your life back, this is how you'll get it."

Shanna gained her balance at the same time she gained her bearings, and headed off down the narrow grassy path she hoped would lead either to her destination or to someplace where someone else could point her in the right direction. At this juncture, there weren't many options. The sun was already getting groggy in the sky, so if she didn't land somewhere soon, the chances looked good for her spending the night out here. Not an appealing thought, sleeping alone in the jungle where who knew what kinds of predators were lurking.

Thing was, the darned bag weighed her down, which slowed her down. But leaving it, maybe coming back tomorrow to get it, wasn't an option. If something happened to it, if it disappeared overnight... She hadn't brought much on this journey, but she wasn't about to do without the few creature comforts she'd included. So she redoubled her efforts, focused only on the trail ahead of her, and bore down for the march. Thinking on every step of it how she was going to explain herself to Ben without looking like an idiot, a total lunatic or both.

A few casual days in a tiny Italian village weren't enough to compel anyone to do what she was doing. Especially given the way those days had gone. He'd been there but, in so many ways, he hadn't been. And that was what she needed to learn from him. How to switch off her feelings and simply get on with it. That's the way he lived his life, being an outstanding doctor, no emotional involvement attached to it. Precisely what she needed to learn. And now she'd traveled halfway around the world to get it, or come to terms with what she would do with the rest of her life if she couldn't. Because heart-on-the-sleeve medicine didn't work in the Brooks medical world.

"Ayúdeme por favor. Mi madre fue mordida por una serpiente. Está muy enferma. No puede mover. Pienso que se morirá. Ayúdeme por favor!"

A young girl, probably no more than ten, appeared on the road and grabbed hold of Shanna's duffel. Not to steal it. Shanna understood that. The child was terrified because, from what Shanna could gather, her mother had been bitten by a snake. *Una serpiente.* Wasn't moving. Possibly dying, or already dead.

"Is she breathing?" Shanna asked instinctively, before she'd had a chance to think that the girl probably spoke no English. *"Respirar. ¿Respira su madre?"* she repeated, grateful for some family urging in the direction of languages.

"Yo no sé. Está en el suelo, como duerme. Pero yo no sé si puede respirar."

Unconscious, on the ground. Status of her breathing unknown. *"¿Sabe donde el hospital es?"* She was asking the girl if she knew where the hospital was.

The girl nodded then pointed straight ahead on the trail.

"¿Es muy distante?" Very far?

The girl shook her head. *"No."*

"Bueno. Por favor, corre al hospital, los dice lo que usted me dijo, y los dice que hay ya un médico con su madre, pero necesitan alguien que puede ayudar a conseguirla al hospital." She was telling the girl to run ahead to the hospital for help,

but the look on the girl's face indicated she either didn't understand or might be afraid to do so. *"¿Lo que es su nombre?"* she asked the girl as they made their way through the grasses.

"Valeria," she said.

"Eso es un hermoso nombre." Beautiful name. *"Agradecimiento."*

Valeria smiled politely with her thank-you, even though she was so scared. Shanna was impressed by the girl's manners, especially given the circumstances. Grace under pressure. Something she needed to master. *"¿Y qué es el nombre de su madre?"*

"Su nombre está Ines."

The mother's name was Ines. Just as that little bit of knowledge sank in, they rounded a clump of tall pampas grass, where Ines was sprawled on the ground. Breathing, thank God! But barely.

Shanna dropped her bag to the ground, knelt to open it, then had second thoughts about snakes. Pit vipers were prevalent here. At least, that was what she'd read on the plane. That, and so many other disjointed facts about Argentina. So she stayed half upright, half bending, and grabbed the few medical supplies she'd been allowed to carry in. No medicines, just equipment. Which wouldn't save the woman's life. *"Soy médico, Valeria. Pero debo ayudar. Por eso yo deseo que vaya al hospital."* I'm a doctor, but I need help.

Back home, help had been at hand with just the push of a button. Out here, she didn't know. And as she wrapped her stethoscope around her neck and clicked on her penlight, she wasn't even sure the kind of help she might have had back home would do much good, given what she was already seeing in Ines.

Truth was, if the bite had come from a pit viper, the only possible treatment was antivenin. *"Debo ayudar."* Yes, she needed help, especially when her first take of the woman's pulse revealed tachycardia. Pulse much too fast and starting to skip some beats. In addition, there was swelling on her left ankle where the bite area was, not only very puffy but red and hot to the touch.

Shanna imagined other symptoms had occurred while the child had waited there with her mother, probably hoping someone would come along to help them—difficulty with speaking, muscle weakness, dizziness before passing out, excessive sweating, blurred vision, maybe even some paralysis.

While she'd never had to treat a venomous snake

bite as a family practitioner, she'd certainly studied them in medical school. Which was nothing like encountering one in front of her. Because what she remembered from her studies was that without fast treatment death followed coma. And the blue tinge developing around Ines's lips was a precursor to death.

"¿Puede correr al hospital, Valeria?" Even though she asked Valeria again to run to the hospital, Shanna wasn't sure it would make much difference. Time was elapsing and she had no idea how long ago Ines had been bitten. But the woman was still breathing, which meant there was still hope. Only at Ben Robinson's hospital, though, and only if Ben stocked the right kinds of antivenin.

The child tugged on Shanna's shirt. *"Sí, puedo. Pero tengo a amigos cerca que puede ayudar a llevar a mi madre allí. Creo que sería más rápido."*

She had friends who could carry Ines there faster. Shanna kept her fingers crossed as she shooed Valeria off to fetch these friends. *"Tan rápidamente como usted puede,"* she urged the child, even though she didn't know if Valeria's fast would be fast enough.

In the meantime, Shanna kept vigil over Ines,

washing the snake wound the best she could with bottled water. There'd been a time when making a tourniquet had been the field standard in care, but studies had proved that when a tourniquet was applied, the poison was likely to concentrate where the tourniquet was cutting off circulation, increasing the chances of amputation or even a faster death.

Then there was the idea that cutting the wound and sucking out the poison could improve things. Unfortunately, too many people had died from sucking the poison into their own lip or mouth cut.

So now she had to sit and wait, feeling as medically ineffective as she had that day when she'd promised her patient, Elsa Willoughby, a kidney transplant. Not a simple thing to promise, granted. But Elsa had been in a bad condition, which should have put her at the top of the list for an available kidney. What she hadn't expected, though, had been the hospital's refusal to allow the procedure once a kidney became available. A refusal that had come from her grandfather, and been upheld by her father and several other doctors bearing the Brooks name. It was like they'd turned into a wall of opposition because she'd had a patient who needed an operation they didn't want to grant.

Your patient is too old, her grandfather had stated. That, and another dozen reasons that had got Elsa rejected from Brooks Medical Center, a conglomerate of three hospitals, nine clinics and fourteen other miscellaneous medical services.

Eventually, the county hospital had taken Elsa, but too late. Her condition had deteriorated to the point that she had no longer been a good enough candidate for a transplant anywhere. She'd gone back on dialysis to await her fate, which had come just four months later.

Shanna still had nightmares about the day she'd had to tell her patient she could do nothing for her, that the medical system she'd loved and trusted had failed her. She'd had a small *breakdown, meltdown,* whatever the term du jour turned out to be. Had spent the night alone, crying, angry, doubting everything about what she was doing.

Next morning she'd gone to her grandfather one more time, trying to persuade him to change his mind. But his was a mind that wouldn't be changed. *"Given your emotional involvement, you may be better suited in an administrative role than the actual practice of medicine,"* her grandfather had said. An administrative role because she cared? It's why she'd left medicine and had gone looking for a better way. Or a different way. Or any way at all that would define her place in medicine. And if it wasn't out there, then what?

Ben Robinson. He proved it was out there. Everything she'd seen of him proved it. And to gain some of what he had, she'd do whatever she had to.

Except here she was again. Not being able to treat a patient. So she spent the next several minutes doing what she'd done with Elsa after she'd broken the news. She sat and held her patient's hand, felt her own pulse jump every time Ines twitched, felt her own breath catch each time Ines's breath went raspy. Heart-on-her-sleeve medicine. Even deep in the jungle she could feel the disapproval of the entire Brooks family.

Luckily for Ines, that wait wasn't long for only minutes after Shanna had settled in she heard quite a clamor coming from the trail. Not just one or two people. Probably not even three or four of them. In fact, by the time she was on her feet, twenty or so people were standing in front of her, hefting a bed. Not a stretcher or some make-shift rig to transport Ines but a single-size bed, mattress, blankets, pillows and all. She'd never seen anything like it. So much response, so much concern… "Put her…" she started to instruct, but the will of the people took over, and before Shanna could blink, Ines was lifted into the bed, and the bed was being whisked down the trail. All she could do was follow.

Which she did, for about half a mile. Then, at the entry to a small wooden building, everybody stepped back for her to go first, after which several of the men followed her in, leaving the bedframe outside and carrying Ines gently on the mattress.

Shanna spotted Ben immediately, and even in the urgency of the moment her heart clutched. Was it excitement to see him, to start her medical makeover? Or was it merely excitement for medical help for her patient? She didn't know which, didn't care. Ben was bent over an empty exam table in what she presumed to be the emergency area. He was adjusting a light, not even aware yet that she was in the room. "Is that table taken?" she asked, smiling when he looked up at her.

"I'm supposing this is not a coincidence, you being here?" Ben asked. He gestured for Shanna to sit down across the table from him. They were in the doctors' lounge, a tiny place with a table, two chairs, an old sofa, a refrigerator and barely enough room to turn around. Sparse of comfort and cramped, but well used by Ben's largely volunteer staff. "Which means you're stalking me, correct?"

She grasped the cup of yerba maté he'd made, a tealike drink popular in Argentina, like it was her lifeline. Ben had mentioned it was his favorite, but she hadn't quite acquired the taste for it yet, like she hadn't yet acquired the taste for the changes she needed to make in herself.

"Believe me, I had thirty hours to think about it on the flight. You know, questions you'd ask. Answers I'd give. What would sound plausible, what wouldn't."

"Plausible would be good," he conceded, still absolutely bewildered by her being there. Wondering, also, if he was hallucinating or under some kind of other spell that plucked his thoughts from his mind and turned them into reality. Because he'd thought about her in every unoccupied moment since he'd left Tuscany. She'd even managed to creep into a few of his occupied moments. And now here she was, like he'd ordered her up and, *poof,* she appeared. "But under the circumstances, difficult. You followed me halfway around the world, and I'm trying to imagine how plausible any explanation for that could be."

"Other than stalking you," she said quite brightly. Taking a sip of the maté, she let the bitter taste mellow out on her tongue for a moment, then nodded as she swallowed. "Which I'm not. At least, not in the traditional sense."

"Okay, then tell me what's the *untraditional* sense." It was flattering that she'd followed him here. At least, he thought it was. Or hoped it was. Because there was the distinct possibility that Shanna Brooks was some kind of lunatic, and he'd completely missed that in her back in Tuscany. Blinded by the aura, oblivious to the reality? No, that didn't make any sense because he'd looked into her eyes more than once, and there was nothing to suggest anything wrong with her. In fact, one of the things he'd been drawn to had been her spark, her vitality, which shone in her eyes.

"It's hard to explain. I…I need something different."

"You needed something different so you stalked me and ended up in my jungle hospital. Which, by the way, isn't on the map, or any global tracking system I know about. So you had to put some effort into finding me." These kinds of things never happened to him, and he wondered if he should pinch himself to make sure he was awake.

Shanna shrugged. "You're right. You're way off the map. But you'd mentioned you were in Argentina, and I'm resourceful. So, here you are." She took another sip of maté, watched him carefully over the top of her mug.

"Yes, here I am." So was she being deliberately vague, or was she as unsure of herself as he was sensing, putting forward the brave front with nothing behind it to back it up? Because Shanna Brooks seemed almost as surprised to be here as he was to see her here. "Several years, now, which gets me back to my original question..."

"Why am I stalking you?" She drew in a deep breath. "The answer is...I want to be like you. So who better to show me how to do that than you?"

Now he was back to the theory that she might be a lunatic. "What you're telling me is that you want to be like a recluse doctor who's running an isolated, struggling volunteer hospital in the middle of a jungle?"

She smiled. "Not sure it does. So you're thinking I'm crazy, aren't you?"

"Probably not crazy enough to medicate you. But odd enough that I might have to keep an eye on you, take away sharp objects, limit your prescribing to sugar pills."

Shanna laughed. "Don't blame you. In the same position, I might also be calling for a security guard."

"If we had one," he said. "Which we don't. So what didn't you tell me back in Tuscany that I obviously should know since you've set your sights on...me?"

"That's a fair question, I suppose."

"Which you're going to answer, I suppose?"

She sat her mug down on the table and simply studied him for a moment. Looked deep into his eyes, never breaking contact for what seemed like an eternity. Then she drew in a deep breath, let it out slowly and smiled. "You deserve an answer, but it's not necessarily the real answer because..."

"Because it's hard to explain," he filled in.

"Harder than you can know."

"Then, start at the beginning."

"The thing is, every story has so many beginnings. With this one, let's begin where medicine and I came to a parting of the ways. For the sake of keeping this brief, let's just call it a discrepancy of idealisms, and move on from there. After I hung up my medical diploma, I went on a road trip. You know, in search of myself, in search of truth, maybe in the higher sense in search of the meaning of life.

"Who knows what I was in search of but, whatever it was, I met you and I liked the way you talked about your medical world. Thought maybe I might like the way you actually deal with it, as well. And I'll admit I probably got caught up pretty easily as I didn't have my own medical world any longer."

"Cutting to the chase," he interrupted. "You followed me here to study me."

"Like I said, it sounds crazy. The only thing I know for sure is that I don't know anything. I loved being a doctor, think I want to keep doing that. But..." She shrugged. "You need volunteers, and I'm here to volunteer."

They hadn't talked about this in Tuscany, and it was something that should have come up when they'd discovered they were both physicians. Of course, how much had he told her about himself? Not much. Shanna had done the same, so he couldn't fault her for that. "Well, you're off to a good start, showing up at my door with your own patient."

"Then you'll let me stay?"

He'd seen good medical skill and that was almost enough to hire her on the spot. But he was cautious about the people he brought in, even if he had spent time with them on holiday. So while his impulses were telling him one thing, his head was still ruling him. It had to because his only priority was Hospital de Caridad. "You show up on my doorstep and declare yourself ready to work, and think I'll just let you start working?"

"I was hoping. And you can do an internet search on me."

"Oh, I intend to." Although what he'd seen of her already told him everything he needed to know. That, and there was no reason to doubt she was who she said she was. Still, those were personal feelings getting in the way, and whatever was going to happen with Shanna had to be kept professional. From here on out she wasn't a wishful memory left over from holiday but one of his volunteers. One of the many who got treated no differently than anyone else. In a way, that was too bad, because he'd like those wishful memories.

"You're a cautious man, Ben Robinson."

"Have to be." He smiled. "You never know who's going to pop out of the jungle and ask for a job."

"Look, I appreciate the opportunity. Just tell me what you want me to do, then point me in the right direction."

He pointed at the door. "Evening house calls. You can come along...observation only for now, just to see how we operate. Then after you're rested..." A sly smile crossed his lips. "And fully checked out, we'll get you on the full schedule." He wasn't sure why he was asking her to tag along, especially as he intended to treat her the way he did all his volunteers—none of whom ever accompanied him on his house calls. Normally, he enjoyed these evening rounds alone, because they got him away from the routine grind and gave him time to walk and think. It was a pleasant way to spend his evenings, yet here he was disrupting himself, and not sure why.

Shanna laughed. "You really don't trust me, do you?"

"You know how that old saying goes, something about keeping your friends close and your stalker closer...."

"Enemies," she corrected. "Keep your enemies closer."

Except he didn't see anything in Shanna that would make her his enemy. If anything, what he saw was…gentle. Compassionate. "For now, let's just keep it at stalker."

"So, do you have a bed for a stalker someplace?" she asked, taking her last sip of mate then pushing back from the table.

Since Amanda and Jack were still occupying the guest cottage until their own cottage was built, and all the volunteer rooms were full, there weren't many options left open. His cottage was built like all the others, two small residences per cottage, divided by a central corridor. As hospital owner, he claimed privilege and took up both residences in his cottage, using one for living and one for storage, because he valued his privacy. Looked like he was going to have to share, though. An idea with a certain jumbled appeal. "I occupy half the cottage around to the side…you walked right past it when you came in."

"Half a cottage?"

"Don't require much."

"So what you're telling me is we're sharing quarters? I'll take the part you don't require?"

"Something like that. You'll get your own room, as well as your own bathroom and a very small living area. So I'll have someone move my things aside and make room for you." Everything in that cottage was the sum total of his life, all of it packed into three or four boxes. Bottom line, there wasn't going to be much of his life to move aside.

"Very practical," she said. "Me being your stalker, and all."

He cleared his throat. "Well, then…" What else was there to say after the most beautiful woman he'd ever set eyes on called him practical? The answer was…nothing. There was nothing to say. Not a word. When a woman saw a man as practical, that was as far as they would go. But that was what he wanted, wasn't it? The two of them going nowhere except on some house calls. Yes, practical was right where he needed to be with her. Right now, though, getting what he wanted didn't feel so good.

CHAPTER THREE

"WHO is she?" Amanda asked, waylaying her brother in the hospital hall and practically shoving him into a supply closet. "And why is she staying in *your* cottage?"

"Technically, the cottages are meant to be shared by two. So she's not really staying in my cottage so much as she's occupying the other half of a cottage that was designed to be used by two people."

"Quit being evasive," Amanda scolded. "I want to know who she is and if she's the one you met in Tuscany. Oh, and why she's here."

"It's not what you think," he told his sister.

"You don't know what I think."

"Yes, I do. It's the same thing you think every time you come up with the crazy idea that I might be getting involved with someone."

"So, are you getting involved with…?"

"Shanna. Shanna Brooks. And, *no*…notice the emphasis I place on the word *no? No,* I'm not getting involved with her. But, yes, she's the person I met in Tuscany."

"And *didn't* have an affair with."

"And didn't have an affair with," he repeated.

"Yet she followed you here?"

"Yes, but I'm still trying to process the reason." Saying she wanted to be like him could be open to so many interpretations. "I think maybe she's just looking for some variety in her medical life."

"Medical life. So she's what? Doctor, nurse, technician?"

"Family-practice doctor. Burned out, I'm pretty sure."

"And she's looking for a nice jungle hospital to rejuvenate her?" Amanda shook her head, smiled. "Don't be naive, Ben. She's looking for *you* to rejuvenate her. Notice the emphasis I place on the word *you*? And I couldn't be happier for you. It's about time you crawled out of your deep, dank hole and did some real living."

"It's a normal hole, and I live just fine in it."

Amanda's curiosity relaxed a bit, and she arched playful eyebrows at him. "Well, whatever it's about, you have very good taste in roommates. In fact, that's a Robinson trait. Just look what happened to me and my roommate." She patted her rounding belly. "It worked out pretty well."

"Because there was something there between the two of you to work out." He held out his hand to stop her from saying the words he knew she'd say. "I'm fine. Just leave it at that, okay?"

"Yeah, well, a beautiful woman just followed you halfway around the world. I'd say that's better than fine, and as for leaving it alone…" Amanda gave her brother an affectionate squeeze on the arm then spun away. "Think I'll go help our new volunteer get settled in."

"She's going on evening house calls with me."

"Like I said, I think I'll help our new volunteer get settled in…later."

"Leave it alone, Amanda," he warned. His sister was a free spirit, which was both endearing and, right this very moment, aggravating.

"According to you, there's nothing to leave alone."

"So let's keep it that way." There were times, though, when he wished he didn't have to.

"You chose a beautiful area," Shanna said, trailing along behind Ben. His long legs kept a brisk pace and while she was tall, just a few inches shy of his six-foot-two frame, with long legs herself, she was struggling to keep up with him.

"It chose me," he said brusquely. "There was a need here, and I had the means to do something about it."

"So you set up a hospital, just like that?" He seemed the type who could. Efficient, not a speck of nonsense in him. She wondered, for a moment, if Ben ever had fun in life, then dismissed the thought when she remembered that her life didn't afford much fun, either. Not even after she'd walked away from medicine and, effectively, everything else in her life. Her goal then had been to see the world, have a good time, forget what frustrated her, what made her angry or sad. Concentrate only on what was good in the moment. Then get back to her life and see how it worked out. This was now the working-out part and fun didn't matter. It was time to be a doctor again but without the emotional involvement that always got in her way.

"Easier said than done. But from a simplistic viewpoint, yes. I set up a hospital just like that. With my sister. She's only just started working here full time, but she's been my partner from the beginning."

"Why Argentina?" Was it easier to fight his demons in such an isolated place? Maybe working so hard with so few resources helped him cope.

"Before you ask, no, it's not about isolating myself from the world because I'm an alcoholic and the temptations here might be fewer. They're not. And I don't consider this isolating myself from the world. My parents were humanitarian workers here for a while. And my sister's native Argentinian, from a region south of here."

"I'd wondered if it might have something to do with your…shall we call it *demon*. But it's not, and—"

"Not, it's not," he interrupted.

"Then I'm glad Argentina comes naturally to you. Choosing where you want to be because it's the right fit or because of the emotional involvement makes your existence there easier. Oh, and just for the record, you overcame a problem, and I admire that. I hope it's not an issue for you, because it's not for me."

"You're the only one I've ever told, Shanna."

"And that's as far as it goes. I hope you'll trust that, because we all have our past mistakes. Believe me, I have my share." Rebelliousness, a husband she never should have married. Definitely a few mistakes there. "But live and learn, or live and wallow. What you're doing here in Argentina isn't wallowing, and that's what matters."

He nodded, seemed to accept that explanation from her, then smiled. "No, being in Argentina isn't about wallowing because I've always loved it here. The people are great, and they're also very appreciative of our efforts—even the little things that don't matter so much in most medical facilities. You know, give them an aspirin for a headache and they're thankful. Back home, you give a patient an aspirin and, well, let's just say it's not likely to be received in the best spirit."

Something she understood completely. Her family employed a cadre of lawyers to keep all things worked out, including the irate patient who might refuse an aspirin for a headache then turn around and sue because she'd wanted a narcotic. As part owner of Brooks Medical Center, Shanna understood that all too well. Which made Ben's set up here seem all the more appealing. "Well, I may need an aspirin for some legs aches if you don't slow down. You're tall, long legs, I'm having a hard time keeping up."

He stopped, measured her up, nodded. "Somehow, I don't think you've ever had a hard time keeping up. In fact, I'm betting that in one way or another you're always out in the lead."

"Not all the time," she said, hearing the sadness starting to slip into her voice. "Sometimes I'm so far behind I'm not sure I'll ever catch up."

Ben stopped. Turned to face her. "Which has nothing to do with our walking pace."

"Nothing." She was surprised by his responsiveness. Had she made a cryptic remark like that to her ex-husband, he wouldn't have caught on. But Ben did. He absolutely did, which tweaked a change in her opinion of him. Made it a little softer in her estimation. And a little less dispassionate.

"If I slow down, are you going to tell me why you want to be like me? I'm not sure I like the idea of being watched that closely."

"Some people might be flattered."

"Or suspicious," he countered.

"Or hanging on by a thread."

"Let me guess. You've come to a crossroad, don't know which way to go, so your choice is to copycat me?" He resumed walking, but much slower this time. "Let me tell you, Shanna. That sounds crazy."

"I know. But all my options at that crossroad are leading me to another career path."

"Then flip a coin."

"Would, if I could. But it's not that easy."

"Sure it is. You're a family practitioner. That seems like a pretty good path to me. So stay on the path you're already on and figure out how to make it work. If you still enjoy practicing medicine."

That was exactly what she was doing, trying to figure out how to make it work. But Ben didn't need to be privy to these things about her, especially the part where she wanted to figure out how to separate herself from the emotion the way he did. Telling him everything would only make him wary and watchful of her weaknesses, the way her grandfather had been.

Here, at Caridad, she had the perfect opportunity to work one on one with the exact kind of doctor she had to become in order to survive—the doctor who didn't flinch or cry when her patient died, or didn't get so emotionally invested she lost sleep, couldn't eat. Her grandfather had called her a sissified practitioner. Her father had backed that up and no one else in her family had come to her defense, which meant they all agreed to some extent, if not totally.

But, then, look at them, the stalwart Brooks family doctors——her parents, grandparents, brothers. Why would they back her up when they were so entrenched in the Brooks family ways? She was the ousted, the one who didn't fit. If she wanted back in, she was the one who had to do the changing. Thing was, she wasn't sure anymore if she really wanted in, and maybe that was what bothered her. However it went, for now, she was exploring options, and Ben was the best option she'd come across. "I love practicing medicine. But for the moment I'm openly observing all paths and leaving it at that." Such a confusing place to be.

"Well, in that case, this path leads to Vera Santos, who had a stroke about a year ago. She gets along fairly well, takes care of her grandchildren during the day when their parents are working, and she has a passion for eating anything and everything that will elevate her blood pressure."

That caught her interest, shook her right out of her confusion. "What medication is she on? Chlorothiazide or furosemide?"

"No medicine. But she's eating more fish and

grain. Garlic, too. And she's currently concentrating on eating more vegetables and fewer sweets."

"Is it working?"

"Marginally. Her blood pressure is still high, but not as high as it was when she had her stroke last year. Which I'd consider progress."

"Progress would be convincing her to take a pill."

"Which she won't do because she doesn't trust our kind of medicine."

"So she doesn't get treated? Her medical condition is like a ticking time bomb, Ben. You know the statistics, she's ten times as likely to have a second stroke because she's already had one and her hypertension isn't controlled. I mean, how can we let that happen?" It didn't seem acceptable, especially with a condition that could kill her. And there she went again, heart on her sleeve and emotional involvement she shouldn't be having.

"She does get treated, Shanna. She's on a better diet, she's losing weight—doing nicely at it, her blood pressure is lowering, and I check her once a week. More, if she's not feeling well. And the big thing is, if she refuses my treatment, and I have offered a variety of options, including pills, I can't force it down her throat."

Ben held the gate open for Shanna, then followed her up the path to the front door. "We deal in realities here. It would be nice to give her a pill, but the reality is, she's allowing me to do only what she wants me to do. It's all I have to work with. I don't like it, because my preference would be something more aggressive. But it's not my preference, so I have to make do and be glad she allows me to do what I'm doing. The alternative could be doing nothing at all."

And there was his practical side, the one that didn't jump in with both feet and get emotionally tangled up at the start. "But she knows the consequences. I tell her every time I see her. Don't like the result, but it's her decision to make, her consequence to deal with."

Shanna knew about choices and consequences. She was living the consequence of her choice now. Somehow, though, losing a family, which she feared was part of what was at stake for her, didn't equate to losing a life, which was exactly what Vera Santos had at risk here—her life. So who really cared that she was already over the emotional edge for this patient? It wasn't like her grandfather was standing there, calling her a sissy for caring. He wasn't. Quite simply, Shanna wanted to help

Vera Santos and that didn't make her a sissified practitioner, no matter what anybody said.

"What if I can persuade her?" she asked. "What if I can get her to agree to take the pills?"

"That sure of yourself?" he asked.

"That sure of human nature." She knocked on the front door, then smiled at him. "And of myself."

"Well, if you're that sure, here's the deal." A mischievous glint popped into his eyes. "You get her to agree to the pills and after house calls I'll show you around the village, take you to dinner at the cantina."

She liked the glint, liked this unexpected side of him because previously, when they had been in Tuscany, he'd never initiated the plans. Whatever they'd done with one another had been more as a result of them mutually stumbling into something together. So Ben asking…that was a nice touch.

"Then get yourself ready for the pay-off, Dr. Robinson," she warned, "because I'm ready for that night on the town."

"But here's the flipside. What do I get in return if she doesn't agree?"

"She'll agree," Shanna said quite confidently.

"But if she doesn't, what's in it for me?"

She thought hard for a moment. "A humble apology for being wrong?"

"Not enough."

His face was totally expressionless and someone who didn't know him might have thought he was being unfriendly. But he wasn't. Ben was reserved but never unfriendly. And that elfish little glint was still in his eyes. "I know you love yerba maté tea, that you drink it every day. What I'll do is brew it and bring it to you whenever you want it, for one entire day. Medical rounds and patient emergencies excluded, of course."

"Tea, but for an entire week, *and* a humble apology. Then the bet's on."

She liked this side of him more and more. Not playful but light in a cautious, grounded sort of way. Like taking the step, but conservatively. Something she needed to learn, actually. "You're a hard man, Ben. But I'm not worried, because I'm going to win," she said as she stepped up to the door to address the woman who had opened it and was now standing there watching the two of them banter.

"*Buenas noches, Sra. Santos,*" Shanna began. "*Me llamo Dr. Brooks. Trabajo en el hospital con Dr. Robinson. La razón que estoy aquí esta noche es que quiero hablar con usted acerca de cómo puede quedarse sano y continuar cuidar de sus nietos."*

"Really?" Ben said. "You're going to use her grandchildren as the reason for her to take her medicine? Isn't that being a little manipulative, telling her you want to talk to her about how to stay healthy so she can take care of them?"

"Not manipulative. Smart." Shanna looked up at him, smiling. "And you're just annoyed you didn't think of it first."

"How do you know I didn't think of it first? Or already tried it?"

"Because, like I said, you're annoyed. If you'd already tried it and it didn't work, you'd be laughing at me. And if you'd tried it and it had worked we wouldn't be making a house call." She stepped through the door Mrs. Santos held open for her, then turned back to Ben. "Is dancing included in that night on the town, by the way?"

His response was to roll his eyes, exaggerate a sigh and follow her inside. No answer, no smile. Faked annoyance, she realized. Which meant his exterior wasn't as hard as she'd thought it was. That came as a surprise. Actually, a huge surprise. But, sometimes she liked surprises.

* * *

"Okay, so you win," Ben said, stepping around Shanna on the path back to the village and doubling his pace. Five house calls, and they were finished for the evening.

"Spoken like a man who's going to grudgingly pay off his wager." She was barely keeping up with him again and, truth be told, she was almost too exhausted to care if he left her behind. Everything about the past few days had finally caught up with her, and the adrenalin edge had worn off. There were no big plans left in her for the rest of the night, except to get back to her room. Forget the tour, forget everything else. All she wanted to do was concentrate on putting one foot in front of the other enough times to get her where she wanted to be—in bed, asleep.

"Spoken like a man who actually wishes he'd thought of your idea first. What you said to convince Vera Santos to take her medicine was nothing short of brilliant. And, yes, I wish I'd thought of it."

"What?" Shanna sputtered, pausing a moment to catch her breath.

Ben stopped and turned around. "You heard

what I said. No need to repeat myself just so you can gloat."

"Only gloat…a little." Suddenly so exhausted she felt paralyzed, her words barely managed to escape her lips.

"Shanna…" He took two steps back toward her but she held up her hand to stop him. "Are you okay?"

"I'm fine. Just a little more tired than I'd expected. Wasn't easy getting here."

"Jet lag, humidity…"

Nodding, Shanna drew in a deep breath. "Is it a rough life out here, Ben?"

"Not particularly. There are differences, but you get used to them."

"I hope so…" Straightening, she started down the path again and had almost caught up with Ben when he turned and continued his own trek, but even at his much slower pace she couldn't keep up. So she didn't even try. Instead, she lagged back and watched him walk. *Man with a purpose,* she thought, noting his long, deliberate strides. *He calculates everything about his life.* Evidenced by his squared shoulders. Not a movement in him without a specific intent. Maybe that was good, all things considered. But she couldn't help wondering if it was also lonely.

Another couple of dozen steps forward, and Ben was totally out of sight, which was just as well because a little cleared patch beside the road called her name. She wanted to sit down. In fact, she dropped her backpack to the ground with that intent, but thought about Ines and the snake then wondered about what other animals might be lurking in the dark, ready to get her.

"Jaguars," Ben said, stepping up behind her. "Cougars, and the occasional boar. Plus the snakes, which you already know about."

Gasping, Shanna spun to face him. "Where did you come from?"

"You weren't keeping up so I rounded back. Saw you contemplating a little rest by the side of the road and figured that if you were as smart as you seem, you were probably wondering what kinds of animals out here might get you if you sat down. Oh, and I originally came from California, if that's what you're asking."

"It's not funny," she snapped. Her heart was pounding so hard it hurt, and she was barely able to breathe, he'd scared her so bad.

"No, being out here alone at night is never

funny. It's one of those differences you have to adjust to."

"Do you routinely take all your volunteers to the jungle at night and scare them to death?"

He chuckled. "Hadn't ever considered it, but it does sound like a good indoctrination idea, doesn't it? Especially since you'll never come this way at night again without being cautious."

He'd actually laughed. Attempted a little humor then laughed. She'd heard it in his voice, wished she could have seen it on his face. "I know I told you you're a hard man, Ben. But I'd like to add cruel to that, as well. You're a hard *and* cruel man. Has anybody ever told you that?"

"Once or twice. But I like to think of myself as a man who doesn't want to see his volunteers get eaten. Which probably wouldn't have happened to you as there hasn't been a sighting of a jaguar near here in years. Still, better to be safe than sorry. Right?"

Not only was he laughing, he was sounding quite chipper. Was this Ben in his element? she wondered. Ben synonymous with the night? Happy in his separation? That analysis didn't seem right. He might put on that dark front—a psychologist would probably say it was meant to keep people away. Yet she saw something else, something behind it, and it wasn't dark at all. In fact, it was quite the opposite. "Did you ever consider that it might be better to warn me rather than scare me?"

"And you're the type who'll listen to a warning? Because you seem just the opposite. You know, the one who has to find out on her own. Learn her lessons the hard way. Confront the jaguar head on to prove there's really a jaguar there."

He was right about that, but she didn't have to admit it to him. "In other words, learn my lesson by getting myself eaten?"

"Why are you really here, Shanna? And don't tell me it's because you want to be like me, because nobody who knows me wants to be like me."

"But I don't know you. All that time we spent together in Tuscany and I really don't know any more than what I see when I look at you."

"That's not why you came to Argentina, to get to know me. And maybe you're here because of that crossroad you've come to. But this is a drastic change from your life, as well as a drastic change from the way you practice medicine. There's nothing here that's easy. Not even the village path."

"Maybe I'm looking for drastic and difficult."

"I'm not buying it. What you're telling me may be partial reasons, but in total I'm not buying it."

"You don't have to. As long as you let me work here, we'll both get what we need. Why complicate it with anything else?"

He shrugged. "Guess we don't have to, do we?" Taking a few steps closer, he bent and picked up her backpack. "Look, it's getting late. I have a couple of patients I want to check on before I grab a of couple hours' sleep, so we need to hurry this along." Then he slid his arm around her waist, clearly for support rather than anything else. "Lean on me and we'll be back at the hospital in a few minutes."

"I'm sorry, Ben. Normally, I have more stamina than this. I really didn't expect to get this tired as I haven't done much of anything for a while now."

"Nothing to be sorry about."

That was all he said. For the rest of the way back they walked in silence. She was glad for the assistance. Snuggling into his side maybe a bit more than she needed to as they walked, she was glad the assistance was coming from Ben.

CHAPTER FOUR

"MY BROTHER thought I should look in on you, and I wanted to meet you…considering what I've heard." Amanda sat a tray of coffee and pastries on the nightstand next to Shanna's bed. "I'm Amanda Kenner, by the way. Part-owner of the hospital and resident pediatrician. And impressed as all get-out that you followed Ben from Italy to Argentina."

"What time is it?" Shanna responded groggily, pushing herself part way to a sitting position. Last night was a blur. Ben had helped her back to the hospital, then she'd practically fallen through the door to her room, and right this moment she didn't have any recollection of tumbling into bed or anything else past the door. Yet here she was, dressed in yesterday's clothes, stretched out in bed and feeling rested. And her only concession to undressing was that her boots and socks were off. Had Ben done that? Had he actually removed them for her?

"It's a little after noon. I'd thought about waking you for breakfast earlier because you missed supper last night, but Ben said you needed sleep more than you needed food, so I waited as long as I could. The thing is, if you're going to volunteer here, I really need you on the work schedule for this afternoon. Normally, we like to give our volunteers a couple of days to acclimatize, but we're in a pinch."

"Sure, I can work." Shanna struggled to a fully upright sitting position, brushed back her hair with her fingers and tried to stifle a yawn. "And about me following Ben here, yes, I did. But it's not what it looks like. I'm not really stalking him."

Grinning, Amanda said, "Well, whatever your reason, we're glad to have you. Caridad is always in need of good volunteers and from what Ben described about your *grand* entrance, you're good. So, about going on duty later..."

She liked Ben's sister. She was as outgoing as Ben was closed in. And Amanda clearly loved her brother. Had some hopeful expectations for him in the relationship department, too, Shanna guessed. "Not a problem. But would you mind if I took half an hour to eat, then grab a shower before I start work? I'm used to putting in the hard hours, but what I've done here so far has been a different kind of hard and I'm a little slow readjusting."

"I'll bet working at your family's medical center was very hard. From my own limited experience of owning Caridad, I know I work longer and harder than I ever did when I was on staff in a hospital back in Texas. Something about the responsibility of ownership that drives us to do more, I think."

"Does Ben know who I am?" she asked, quite alarmed. Leading off with her family and their medical empire wasn't something she was comfortable with, so she didn't. In fact, it never came up in conversation unless the other person asked, because she'd learned, early on, that being the youngest child of a medical dynasty carried a stigma of sorts. Or unrealistic expectations. Sometimes it simply put a target with a bull's eye on her forehead. *Look at me.* She hated that notoriety. Hated the attention because for her, her motivations weren't about being part of the illustrious Brooks family. They were about being a doctor. And while the two should have been one and the same, so often, it seemed, they weren't. Not to her, anyway. Although the rest of the family would dispute that.

"Yep, he knows who you are. Told me where to look you up, actually. But as you didn't know he knows, I'd better warn you, in case it comes up, that my brother applied for a residency at your hospital."

That surprised her. "He was a resident there?" She didn't recall him, didn't recall seeing anything in his brief online bio about him working there, didn't even recall his name from back in the day, and she and Ben should have, at the very least, crossed paths for a year or two in one hospital hall or another as she was thirty-four and he was only a couple of years older.

"No, he wasn't. He just applied for the position. And was rejected."

Shanna opened her mouth to speak but didn't know what to say. "How?" she finally managed.

A passing sadness crossed Amanda's face, followed by a smile. But not the cheery smile that had been there. "Bad attitude. Impeccable academic credits, medical aptitude that couldn't be touched by anyone else. But a pretty big chip on his shoulder. Don't worry about it, though. He eventually landed at a hospital in New York City that was a much better fit for him.''

Odd revelation. She didn't know what to make of it. "So, how do I react to that?''

"You don't. Ben doesn't carry grudges.''

"Then I guess I should say that's a relief because I want to stay here for a while.''

"It's a relief only if you want long, hard hours, no pay and lots of bugs," said Amanda as she swatted a mosquito on her arm. "Which is probably what you'd get at Brooks Medical Center, minus the no pay and bugs. *Especially the bugs.*''

"Money's not a problem, and bugs I can deal with. I liked entomology when I was in college. Used to torment my brothers with bugs instead of the other way around. Always found it was a good way to get even with them…drop some kind of bug in one of their shoes, put something crawly in a school backpack." Smiling at the memory, she scooted to the edge of the bed, picked up the cup of coffee and took a sip.

"Now I feel human again," she said on a sigh.

"Ben and I didn't torment each other so much as conspire together. We were always out to conquer something…mostly the kids who lived down the street. They were bullies. Maybe not in the literal definition of how we see bullies today, but they called us names, threw things at us, ganged up to keep us from walking by their house. So Ben and I were allies early on."

"That's nice," Shanna said wistfully. "My family was never close. Everybody was…busy. Stodgy. They worked, didn't have much time to stay home. Consequently, John, Adam and I were raised by a very caring nanny who tried hard but who couldn't quite instill in us that sense of family. So we weren't close the way you and Ben were, and I think because I was the youngest I was the one who was always trying to get noticed the most. Hence the bugs."

"Family dynamics," Amanda said, patting her tummy. "I'm beginning to see them from the other point of view."

"And it's good?" Shanna already knew the answer. Amanda had the contented look of a woman who had it all. A look to envy.

"Like nothing I would have ever imagined. Anyway, take an hour. Get yourself up and ready for work, then have a look around the hospital. I've got you scheduled for our Emergency, which isn't really much of an Emergency. But it gets busy, and we're down one doctor until my husband gets back..."

"Jack Kenner, right?"

At the mention of his name Amanda smiled from ear to ear. "You know who he is?"

Shanna nodded as she took her next sip of coffee. "He's a big deal in epidemics. We had a situation once at Brooks Medical Center, tried to get him to come and figure it out. He was tied up in Africa somewhere, dealing with malaria. My grandfather offered him an insane amount of money to drop what he was doing and come and help us. Wanted to send the family jet to get him. But your husband had integrity. Stayed where he was." One more sip. "Can't wait to meet him, and it'll be an honor to step in for him."

"I expect Ben will step into Emergency to check on you. But if he doesn't, I'll have one of the nurses help get you situated."

As it turned out, getting situated was an understatement. An hour later, when Shanna entered the room designated as Emergency, she was besieged by patients, dozens of them surrounding her immediately, wanting to see her, trying to tell her what was wrong, trying to grab her attention first. The doctor on duty, a small, thin, older man by the name of Vance Hastings, looked like he was about to become one of the patients himself.

"Getting too old for this," he wheezed as he dabbed his forehead with a handkerchief. "Ten-hour shifts at this pace are for the young." He finally managed a smile at Shanna. "But if you need help, I might have another hour or two left in me."

Shanna chuckled. "How about I prescribe bed rest for now, and if I need you later on, I'll come and get you?"

"Bless you, my child. You've just saved an old man's life."

His friendly smile was nice, very soothing. Yet she wondered why he pushed himself so hard when it was so clearly difficult on him. How difficult, she couldn't have even begun to guess until the end of her first hour on shift, when she'd already seen ten patients and was beginning to question if she'd be able to hold out for another nine hours.

"It's overwhelming, isn't it?" Ben said, stepping into the cubicle where she'd just dressed and bandaged a little girl's foot and sent her back to her mother's arms.

"Is it like this every day?" she asked, leaning against the wall, trying to take a two-minute break.

"Some days it's worse."

"So, conversely, some days it's better?" she asked.

"No, not usually. At least, not during summer. People are active, they get hurt more, other weather-related things pop up. It'll slow down when the weather cools, though. Not that you'll be around long enough to see that."

"Big assumption to make, isn't it? Especially when I stalked you halfway around the world just so I could do what I'm doing."

To help her, he pulled the paper cover off the exam table and replaced it with a fresh one, then set about the task of restocking the table-side tools. "It's also a big assumption to make, thinking you'll want to stay that long. I'm a boring man, Shanna. I work and that's it. So once you've started to observe what you think you want to observe in me, what you're going to find is…nothing. And if this fascination with me is the only reason you're here, you'll be long gone before the cool weather hits."

"But what if I'm not, Ben?"

"Are you challenging me to another wager? Because this is the one you'll lose."

"If I lose, I'm your yerba maté tea slave for the duration of my stay, whatever that turns out to be—I'll give you adequate notice if I leave, by the way. And if I win, the first thing I want is a humble apology. Next thing is my morning coffee served to me in bed. Amanda did that for me this morning and it was nice, so I want a morning coffee slave for the duration of my stay."

"Which is going to be over long before cold weather strikes." He smiled. "No matter how adequate your notice is."

"Do you want me to leave?" It seemed like he might, but she wasn't sure. Then she saw it, the distance in his eyes replaced by that glint. It was his giveaway, she realized. A little tease, an invitation to advance, but only a little.

"I never like to lose a good doctor. But I have an idea Brooks Medical Center never likes to lose a good doctor, either. Especially one who comes with the Brooks name."

"How long have you known?"

"I did an internet search before I took you out on house calls. Back in Italy, unraveling your curious background didn't seem necessary because it had nothing to do with my hospital. And going for six days without telling me you're a doctor is curious, Shanna. But the moment you invaded my Emergency it not only became necessary to find out about you, but urgent, given your intention to volunteer.

"Yet you didn't say anything to me?"

"And yet I didn't say anything. People are entitled to their privacy, Shanna. Everybody, including Shanna Brooks, who was made assistant head of family practice only days before she left. Or, as the hospital's public statement put it, went on an extended personal leave for rest and relaxation before assuming her next level of duties. The thing is, I figured if you wanted me to know who you were, you'd tell me. You didn't, so I didn't see any point in worrying about it."

"We had a difference of opinion—my grandfather and I. Over a patient's treatment. As a result, I realized I had some thinking to do, and I couldn't do it and still continue to work."

"Did you go against the status quo?"

"Tried to. At the time I didn't even realize that's what I was doing. My patient was in end-stage renal disease, I put her on the transplant list. My grandfather took her off because she was older than the hospital protocol called for. I argued, he won, she died."

Ben whistled softly. "I'm sorry. It's always tough when you can't do anything."

"It's even tougher, Ben, when you're part-owner of a family business and the family turns against you."

"You took it personally?"

"Yes, I did. Very personally. I should have been able to save my patient. Her family expected that of me, I expected that of me." She shut her eyes, trying to blot that day from her memory—the day she'd told Elsa the bad news. Heart on her sleeve all the way, and she didn't care. Alone in her office afterward, she'd cried, kicked the trash can. Been called weak by her grandfather. *Do you think you're going to survive in this profession, Shanna, if you're weak?*

Weak. That one, single word had forced her decision. "It's like there's always been this undertow, something churning underneath the surface waiting to pull me under. I always fight hard against it. I was fighting hard against it for my patient, but..." She shrugged.

"I wasn't strong enough when I should have been. So it took me a few weeks to tie up all my medical loose ends, then I went to Tuscany for a holiday, to think… My family has a home there and it seemed like a safe place to be. And the rest, as they say, is history. Here I am." Yes, here she was, wondering if she ever could be strong enough to survive as a doctor or if her emotions would always get in the way.

"Here you are, and Caridad is glad to have you. But I'm wondering if you should have stayed at Brooks Medical and worked it out, rather than coming here."

"The problem is me, Ben. Not Brooks Medical Center. And, no, I couldn't have worked it out there, couldn't have worked *me* out there. But don't worry. I'm not going to jeopardize anything at Caridad. Not going to let my problems overshadow my work. Not going to suddenly figure out which path to take and leave you in a lurch. If that's what you're thinking." If he wasn't, he should be. But she hoped he wasn't, because what Ben thought about her mattered. She wasn't sure why, exactly. She only knew that it did.

"I didn't think you would."

"What makes you so…trusting? If a doctor came to me the way I came to you, I wouldn't do what you've done."

"It's not that I'm trusting. I just don't expect anything from anybody. That way, whatever happens happens. And I don't get disappointed. That's as far as I let anything go. The way I want to live my life, and I'm happy with it."

That might be the way he lived his life, and maybe he was happy with it, but why did she see a distant sadness in his eyes so much of the time? Could it be this wasn't the way he wanted to live his life but the way he thought he had to?

"Anyway…" She pointed to the adjacent room, one half the size of the closet-size room in which she was working "I noticed it's set up for patient care. If you're not busy right now, would you care to see a few patients in there rather than letting that space go to waste?"

"Spoken like a doctor who's used to being in charge," he said, smiling.

"Not as in charge as I used to think I was." She turned then headed to the door, on her way to the hall to call her next patient. "Tomorrow night good for you?" she tossed over her shoulder on her way out.

"For what?"

"Dinner. You still owe me that night on the town, and I'm ready to collect. I'm scheduled for a back-to-back today and tomorrow, which means by tomorrow evening I'll be free." She spun to face him, not expecting him to be so close on her heels—so close they could have kissed. "So, dinner?" It was the first time she'd really noticed the extent and severity of the scars on his neck. Oh, she'd seen them, hadn't paid too much attention. But this close she knew that what was visible on Ben was only a small part of it. She also knew the suffering that had come with them.

"Barring medical emergencies, mud slides and pestilence, I think I might be able to manage dinner," he replied, stepping back from her.

She laughed. "I've never had pestilence used as an excuse to stand me up."

"Not stand you up per se. Just warning you that if pestilence happens…" Rather than finishing his sentence, he brushed by her and went to the waiting area and called the next patient, while Shanna stood back and watched. Beautiful man, amazing physique, accentuated by the fact that this was the hospital where they didn't have to wear scrubs and white jackets if they didn't want to. Ben was dressed in a casual pair of tan cargo pants, along with a baggy camp shirt, long sleeves rolled up to just below the elbows. He exercised, kept himself in superb shape, which was evidenced in the muscles that rippled underneath all that fabric. Brown eyes, casually shaggy brown hair...the substance of dreamy sighs, she thought.

Yes, he was definitely a guy who could make a girl go giddy with his good looks. But he was locked up so tight. Maybe because of his scars, maybe because of something else. Which really didn't make a difference, or shouldn't make a difference. She was only here to learn from him, and not get goose bumps from just looking at him.

Shanna followed Ben to the waiting area to call her next patient, brushing her arm, trying to rid herself of her goose bumps.

Time passed so quickly she felt like her head was swimming. One minute she was in the middle of yesterday's shift, now it was the end of the next day, she'd worked twenty hours out of the last thirty, and every single one of them had gone by in a blur.

Even more amazing was the fact that she'd never worked as hard in her whole life, or felt so good about her accomplishments. Little things. Sore throat. Bug bites. Cuts. Sprains. Pregnancy checks. All of that, and her body wasn't protesting...yet.

Of course, she could be on an adrenalin kick, or maybe it was the evening ahead with Ben that was giving her this late burst of energy.

Either way, she was charged, raring to go.

The funny thing was, she hadn't been out on a date of any sort in, what? Definitely not since the divorce five years ago. Add two years of marriage to that, most of which she hadn't even lived with her husband…now that she'd done the math, she was suddenly nervous. Which showed itself when Ben knocked on her door and her reaction was a little clutch in her heart and a little catch in her lungs. Then that last quick look in the mirror to make sure she was presentable, even though Ben had already seen her covered in the best the jungle had to offer.

"It's not a date," she said aloud as she dabbed on a bit of lip gloss, ran her fingers through her hair to give it just a little more wild edge and headed to the door. "He's paying off a bet." Doing the honorable thing.

"I have to be back on duty in an hour," he said, right off.

Her formerly clutching heart sank a little, but she smiled through it. "And I have a date with a riveting medical journal, so that works out, doesn't it?" A reactionary riposte, she knew, but it was the best she could come up with.

"Then I guess we'd better hurry." Ben didn't come in. Instead he stepped back from the door and actually started to walk down the corridor. Not as an escort, but as someone to follow.

"I guess we had. You go on ahead, and I'll catch up." With that, Shanna dashed back into her room, grabbed a tissue and wiped the gloss off her lips, then found a rubber band. When she caught up to Ben, who was halfway off the hospital compound, her hair was pulled back into her workaday ponytail.

And he didn't say a word about it. Not one darned word. In fact, he barely spoke as they walked down to the village, not hand in hand. Not even together, as his pace was always about two steps in front of her. The place where he seemed to want to be.

Then, apart from the expected conversation—*it's a nice night, we're having nice weather*—the other little bits of conversation focused on patients and hospital supplies, and by the time they reached the edge of the village proper, Shanna was so annoyed by his rude behavior she blurted out, "How about we just skip this whole thing, since it's obvious you don't want to do this?"

Ben stopped a good five feet ahead of her but didn't turn to face her right away. In fact, it took him several seconds before he spun around. "It's not that I don't want to do this. It's that I *don't* do this."

"What? Take a night off?"

"No. I don't take women to dinner. Or anywhere else, for that matter. Remember how I told you I was boring? Remember how we simply met up in Tuscany but never really went together? Well, this is part of it. I *do not* date. Not ever."

This was something she hadn't seen coming. Not at all. "Because you don't like women? You're gay?"

He actually laughed. "I love women. The only gender for me, actually. But I don't get involved with them."

"How would you define involved? Because in my world a one-hour night out on the village doesn't constitute an involvement."

"Especially in a ponytail?" he asked.

Now she was perplexed. Noticing her quick hair change would indicate a signal of some sort. She just didn't know what kind of signal. More than that, she didn't know what kind of signal she wanted. Because, like Ben, she didn't get involved, and she had a divorce certificate to remind her just how messy an involvement of a personal nature could be. "You noticed?"

"I'm not oblivious, Shanna. Maybe a little obtuse in some matters, but I do notice the things around me."

"Obtuse by design," she commented, even though she was still keeping her distance.

"Not denying it."

Well, at least he was honest. No way she could fault that. "As long as we know where we stand," she said.

"See, that's the thing. You may know where you stand, but I don't. I don't even know why you're here. The real reason. Not the one you're giving me."

"And that bothers you?"

"What bothers me is that I planned an hour for this dinner, and we're standing in the middle of the road, wasting it."

See, there it was again, the nagging reminder that Ben didn't want this. And it wasn't only about dinner. Which made her wonder how she was going to stay close enough to watch him when all he wanted was to keep her at a distance. She'd hoped something would come of this evening, even if he'd reduced it to mere minutes.

Now, though, it felt like he was even shutting that down to her, so what was the point of continuing when it was obvious his conversation would not go much beyond the weather or the patient with severe eczema? "You know what, Ben? You're off the hook. I relieve you of your obligation to take me to the village. You can have your hour back, okay? Have fun with it."

With that, she spun around and marched as hard and fast as she could back to her room, where she slammed the door, kicked a wooden footstool across the small confines, then threw herself down on the bed and simply stared up at the ceiling.

Okay, so maybe she did let her emotions get in the way. And maybe he wasn't the one, and this wasn't the place. But she wasn't ready to concede that her grandfather was right about her, because that doomed her to a career she simply didn't want. Even thinking about spending every day pushing papers and fiddling with mundane business things made her queasy. That wasn't her idea of being a doctor, but it was all her family was offering unless…

"Unless I learn to be more like Ben and less like me." That reality caused a hard lump to form in her throat. Being like Ben wasn't a victory. It was a concession. "Just do it, Shanna," she said, staring so intently at the lovely little *mariposas*—butterflies—taking up residence on her ceiling light that a bang on her door startled her.

"Go away," she shouted, knowing instinctively it was Ben coming to make amends.

"By my watch, I still have a little over half an hour coming to me," he shouted back.

"Consider it my gift to you. And don't you dare tell me you've marked it down in your calendar and you can't change it."

"I did. It's in ink, so it's impossible to change," he countered.

In spite of herself, she laughed. Ben Robinson might have the social skills of a pink fairy armadillo, an Argentine animal that possessed the ability to bury itself completely in a matter of seconds if frightened, but Ben's armadillo ways were engaging in some respects. "If you promise not to bury yourself in the dirt the instant you step inside, the door's unlocked. Come in, if you want to."

"I'm not sure…was that an invitation?" he asked, pushing the door open.

"If you want it to be." Surprisingly, she wanted him to open that door.

"Look," he said, stepping over the threshold yet not entering the room, "I live a very secluded life out here, forget how things are supposed to work sometimes."

"Like common civilities?"

He nodded. "I, um… No excuses. I was rude and I'm sorry. I so totally avoid all the social trappings that I forget how people might have certain expectations of me in those areas, since I don't have expectations of myself. I didn't mean to offend you, Shanna. In fact, I was looking forward to—"

"An hour," she interrupted.

"Okay, you're going to get another apology because I realize that timeline was uncalled for. That was me, trying to play it safe."

"Safe from what?" she asked, sitting up and scooting to the edge of the bed. "From me? Do you think I have *those* kinds of intentions? You know, follow you all the way from Tuscany to wherever in the world this is just to seduce you? Because if it was seduction I wanted from you, I'd have gotten it over with in Tuscany, and right now I'd be sipping wine in a Paris bistro instead of lying in my bed watching bugs in Argentina."

"What else am I supposed to believe? You tell me you're here so you can be like me, and if that's the case then you're certifiably insane. And I don't think you're insane."

"I need a new dedication in my life, Ben, and I wasn't finding it where I was. You intrigued me in Tuscany and that's why I came here. The kind of dedication you have is what I want to develop in myself." Dedication, meaning *dispassion* or *distance*. Which she would never, ever say to him in those terms because that would be hurtful. Ben didn't deserve that.

He shook his head. "All I see when I'm watching you work is dedication. You're involved, Shanna. And passionate. How can that *not* be dedication?" He stepped into the room, took a few more steps forward, then extended his hand to her. "Anyway, let's not ruin the rest of the evening with philosophical conundrums. Come on, get up. I owe you a dinner."

She looked at his hand for a moment. Soft, gentle. The kind of hand that could stroke a woman into easy submission. "I'll go, but only because it's in ink on your calendar and, God only knows, you can't change it once it's in ink."

"I wrote it in ink because I didn't want to find an excuse to get out of it."

"But an hour?" she asked, taking hold of his hand and tingling to everything she'd expected his touch to be. Tingling *and* goose bumps.

"That gave *you* your out, Shanna. I'm not the most engaging person to be around so I figured an hour was time enough to eat and for you to make a polite exit once you realized that anything more than an hour with me would turn into misery. So, yes, an hour. But let's add an option to that."

"An option for what?"

"More. There's nothing written in ink underneath that hour."

"So I get to negotiate for another hour if the first one goes well?" Normally, this was where she'd have simply shoved him out the door, by brute force if necessary, then locked it after him. But she did have those tingles and goose bumps to contend with, whatever they meant. Besides that, Ben fascinated her. His odd outlook on life could be her starting point.

"If you want to negotiate. Not sure that's going to happen, though."

"Pretty sure you're that boring, are you, Doctor?" she asked, standing. "Do I feel another wager coming on? Because I like to dance, so it might involve a tango. Just thought I should warn you."

What was it about her that intrigued him? She was pretty. Downright beautiful, actually. Red hair like he'd never known red could be. Sensual, soft. And green eyes the color of emeralds. So, in spite of his empty heart, there were so many reasons to look. He was human after all. But what else? Her infectious personality? Because Shanna had the ability to draw people in, and he wasn't denying that he'd been drawn in, starting with that first morning in Tuscany when she'd approached him and he'd walked away.

And too many stray thoughts long after that. Now, thinking about the two of them in a tango, specifically a sultry Argentine tango…he could almost feel her leg snaking up his, feel her thigh pressed to his.

When he realized where his thoughts were taking him, Ben expelled a sharp breath. No way in hell that was going to happen. He wouldn't allow it. And that was where his mind stayed for a good part of their walk to the village—on the things he wouldn't allow.

Except the list was provocative, because everything he forbade himself was everything he wanted, and the more he tried to force it away, the more it pummeled him. It was only when they were seated across from each other at the *restaurante aéreo fresco* and Shanna was studying the menu scribbled on a chalkboard hanging on the outside brick wall that he was able to force himself to relax a little. Otherwise he was well into his second chance at an evening he didn't want to ruin, on the verge of ruining that, too.

"If I could make a recommendation, *bife a caballo* is excellent. Beef is the traditional evening meal here, and *a caballo* means—"

"On a horse?" she asked.

"I forgot you speak the language."

"Some. It was the second language in my home when I was growing up."

"I'm guessing a Spanish-speaking nanny?" He smiled as he flagged down the server, a young girl who didn't look to be more than fifteen or sixteen. Glancing back to acknowledge him, she was moving slowly, holding her back. Looked exhausted, so he gave her the okay sign and a smile, indicating he wasn't in a hurry.

"Best nanny in the world—one of the Brooks family perks."

"Spoken with a hint of disdain."

"Not disdain so much as disappointment. I love Asuncion. Would trust her with my own child, if I had children. The thing is, I would raise my own children and not leave that to the nanny. Her job would be as caregiver when I wasn't there, not stand-in parent. But when I was growing up, she was my stand-in parent because my parents were so involved in the hospital. I'd go days without even seeing them. Wouldn't even see them when they were home."

"I met your father the day your grandfather rejected me for a residency position. He was…formidable. Not much separation between your father and your grandfather, actually."

Shanna tensed. "I'm sorry you were rejected, Ben. My grandfather is a very hard man. He has his ideas and he doesn't budge."

He reached across the table, squeezed her hand. "But I benefited from his rejection because I found a hospital that taught me what I needed to know about surviving in the kind of practice I've set up here. It was rough, but it was also good, so I should probably thank your family for turning me down because your grandfather was correct when he told me my personality was abrasive and I was too argumentative to succeed in their residency program."

"Were you really abrasive and argumentative?" she asked. "Because I can't see that. Socially distant bordering on cold or aloof maybe. But abrasive and argumentative?"

He chuckled. "Talk about abrasive."

She smiled. "Sometimes the truth is harsh. But that's how I see you…most of the time. It's not a criticism, though."

"It's not harsh. The truth is the truth, but it's not always so nice to hear. Anyway, back then I was abrasive and especially argumentative. Lots of axes to grind, I suppose. And it's still in me, if I want it to be."

"Do you want it to be?"

"Not for a long time. Behaving that way doesn't prove anything and, in the end, the only one truly hurt is yourself. So why bother when it doesn't get you what you need?"

"What do you need?"

"A tiny hospital in an isolated area of Argentina."

Shanna sighed, slipped her hand out of his and relaxed back into her chair. "I'm still sorry my grandfather rejected you, but I'm glad you got everything you wanted in spite of him."

"One of life's little ironies is that I didn't get what I wanted at the time, but what I needed found me when I was ready for it. It worked out the way it was meant to." But it wasn't all good with her. He could see it in her eyes, in the way her shoulders went so rigid. Her new *dedication* had something to do with her family, and it was about a lot more than an argument over the treatment of an end-stage renal patient. Asking her about it would signal involvement, however, so he opted for the safe route.

He deferred back to the menu. "Anyway, *bife a caballo* is a steak topped with a couple of fried eggs, with fried potatoes and salad on the side. It was a traditional meal before the gauchos set out on their horses to tend to their ranch—hence the equine reference in the name. Not what I'd care to eat before I go horseback riding, but to each his own, I suppose."

"Sounds…huge. But I like food, so it'll work."

"*Bife a caballo.* Make that two," he said, holding up two fingers to the young server, who'd finally made her way to the table, seeming awfully glad to stand there and rest while he and Shanna talked. "With lemonade?" he asked Shanna. Then confirmed it to the server when Shanna said yes. "*Dos vasos de limonada también, por favor.*"

"So now that the dinner necessities are taken care of, and I've apologized on behalf of my family, although I doubt they'd actually ever apologize to anyone about anything, is this where we discover we have nothing to talk about, or so many things in common we won't be able to stop talking?"

"The former for me," Ben said. "Keeps it simple."

"What's wrong with making it complicated?"

"Complicated takes too much effort. There's too much responsibility involved, and I have enough of that with the hospital. Don't care to go looking for more."

"Makes sense to me," she said, knowing it did but simply not feeling the substance of it. "So, in the spirit of simplicity, how about we come up with a list of complicated topics we're not going to talk about? You know, set our boundaries?"

"Sounds like something I'd say."

"I know," she said. "Isn't that great? Since you recognized it, that means I passed my first test at being like you!"

"Are you always this direct?" he asked.

"No, but that's one of my off-limits subjects."

"Like why you're here is?"

She stared at him point-blank. "I already told you why I'm here."

"And I told you I don't believe you."

"So, let's add that to the list. Also my family, and my family's hospital."

"Which would all be interrelated with your reason for setting limits on what we can talk about, I'm guessing. And that's probably off limits, too." She was different. Fresh. He liked the honesty, even if it was a bit quirky and definitely brutal.

"You're right. Off limits."

"Which pretty well limits us to medicine."

"And the weather," she added, smiling. "I'm always up for a good, rousing discussion on heat and humidity."

"Unless it's one of my off-limits subjects." Said with a deadpan face.

"In which case, I'll talk about this really advanced case of lupus I treated in one of my patients a while back, and what happened when we—"

He thrust out his hand to stop her. "*We* would imply your medical colleagues or your hospital, and I don't want you breaking any of your conversational boundaries. Just trying to stick to our rules of engagement."

"So, in these rules of engagement, medicine's basically out?"

He faked a frown. It was silly chatter, he knew that, but it was the first time he'd just let himself go in a conversation other than with Amanda and Jack in so long he couldn't remember. With Shanna, it was fun. Nonsense, but fun. "Not out, totally. But I think we'll have to be very careful how we proceed." Very careful, indeed.

CHAPTER FIVE

"You barely touched it," Ben said as the server was clearing the table of dishes. "If you didn't like it, I'm sure there's something else on the menu…"

Laughing, she held out her hand to stop him. "That's not it. Everything was delicious. But they served me enough to feed a family of four for a week. How's anybody supposed to eat that much?" Shanna glanced over at his plate, saw it was empty. Practically licked clean. She shrugged a fake wince.

"Except you, apparently. And, might I add, I'm impressed, unless you have the metabolism of a bird. In which case, I'm still impressed, but not as much."

"I think I skipped a couple meals today, maybe one or two yesterday, probably all of them the day before."

"Sounds like you need a keeper." Which sounded way more involved than she'd intended it to. Of course she was safe on the domestic count, being a woman who'd never cooked a complete meal in her entire life, to the annoyance of her ex-husband, who'd wanted both professional status as well as a domestic diva in his little woman.

"Or maybe I could simply use four more hours in the day, with an extra day tagged on at the end of the week."

"Four more hours and one more day in which you'd forget to eat. So, I have a question."

"Off limits?"

"Shouldn't be, but I don't really know since we never got around to discussing what's off limits for you. Anyway, it's about Tuscany. You don't seem like the type of person who'd ever want to take a holiday, yet there you were, all relaxed..."

"Until you sat down at my table."

"That *did* disrupt you, didn't it?" she said with a smile.

"Not as much as looking up and seeing you standing there in my emergency room a few weeks later."

"Unavoidable. Both times, actually. You were sitting at the table I'd sat at every morning for a month, and I didn't want to miss my view. It's spectacular. Something I looked forward to. And there was nothing I could do about barging into your Emergency because I had a dying patient and yours was the only Emergency in a hundred miles. Anyway, back to Tuscany. What was that about? Because men like you who won't take time off to eat also won't take time off to go skiing."

"It was about a Christmas gift from my sister and her husband. We'd had a stressful few months, learning things about our parents we didn't want to know. Amanda and her husband had their time away when they married and they thought I needed some downtime, as well. I'm not so much of a recluse that I could turn it down. Besides, I'd always wanted to go to Tuscany."

"I wouldn't have guessed you for the Tuscany type."

"Me neither, actually. But even now and then even someone like me has a need for something nice."

"Ben, I didn't mean…" Too late. The moment her words were out, that little bit of abandon she'd caught a glimpse of in him retreated to distant icebergs. Now there he was, all rigid and brooding, just like the way he'd been that morning in Tuscany. In other words, her evening with Dr. Ben Robinson had ended the way it had started. Badly.

"I'm sorry. I didn't mean to imply you wouldn't want something nice, like a holiday in Tuscany."

"You're right, though. It wasn't me. It was the person who stepped outside me for a few days."

"We create who we want to be, Ben. That's the easy part. The hard part is figuring out who that is. And I liked the man I met in Tuscany, otherwise I wouldn't have spent time with him. But I like the man in Argentina, as well. He's different. Not as relaxed. Underestimates himself in huge ways, but every bit as likeable as the man I met in Tuscany when he wants to be…which isn't enough."

"When he wants to be. See, that's the crux of the matter, isn't it? I don't really care if I'm liked as a person. Being respected as a doctor is more important, and as often as not it's easier not being liked."

"Really? You're serious?"

He shrugged. "I'm not a disagreeable person, Shanna. At least, I try not to be. But as far as extending myself so someone can like me, or be my friend…it doesn't matter. Being alone is fine. I'm used to my own company, and I can accept that."

"Because of your scars?" she asked, and instantly regretted it, because he tensed up. The strain was obvious at once in his face, in the way he squared his shoulders and sat up straighter in his chair. "Or is that an off-limits topic?" she asked quickly,

"My scars have nothing to do with anything and, yes, I prefer not to talk about them."

His voice couldn't have been any stiffer. And just like that, their evening together was over. He distanced himself and she could see he wasn't coming back around anytime soon because he was exhibiting all the telltale signs—looking around, glancing at his watch, huffing out impatient sighs.

She hadn't meant to turn a pleasant time into one where half the people involved didn't want to tolerate the other half, and it was painfully obvious Ben didn't want to tolerate her right now. Fighting himself not to show it, and losing the fight.

"Okay, I'll add it to the list. Anyway, I, um…I need to get back. Reading to do… And sleep. Lovely dinner, though. Very…" She stood, pushed the chair back so hard it toppled over, hitting the plank floor with a hollow thud. One of the servers pushed through the crowded tables to right the chair, and she was grateful for the distraction as Ben was simply sitting there, staring at her, so untouchable on any level that all she wanted to do was get away. "Thank you," she managed, after the server had scooted away.

"Wouldn't you care to stay and have dessert or coffee?" he asked, trying hard to force pleasantries into the clumsy moment.

"If I go now, I can read one journal article and still have ten hours of uninterrupted sleep before I'm back on duty. Win-win for me." She smiled, but the sentiment behind it was…well, she wasn't sure. Let down, maybe?

Finally, he stood. "Look, I'm sorry this is so awkward. Like I told you, I don't do this, Shanna. Don't go out, don't socialize. Don't have pleasant conversations with beautiful women. Now you see why."

"What I see, Ben, is a man who holds himself back. If that's your choice, then it's your choice. But if you're doing it because you think your scars really matter to me, or because you believe you can't socialize or you're not good at it, you're wrong. Because I did have a lovely evening *with* you, up until the moment you decided to check out of our date because I mentioned something that was, apparently, on your list. You underestimate who you are, Ben. And you underestimate how people view you."

"Or I know how people view me, and I've put myself in a place where it doesn't matter anymore."

"It matters, Ben. And I'm sorry for your isolation. So now I'm going back to my room. Please, stay here. Have your dessert and coffee. Don't worry about me. I'll be fine getting back on my own." It wasn't the worst date she'd ever had. That would have been the one where she'd met her ex-husband—a night of business transactions, pure and simple. Oh, he'd been charming enough. Hadn't checked out on her like Ben just had. But he hadn't really been there, either. Probably because he had been daydreaming his way to Chief of Surgery at Brooks, a sure promotion when you married the collective owners' daughter, grand-daughter, sister, whatever you wanted to call her. The thing was, that bad date had ended in marriage two months later. This one…it wasn't going to end in anything. Ben wore his intentions looped around his neck the way he did his stethoscope.

On her way down the road Shanna glanced back at Ben, who was paying the server and probably thinking about the faster path back to the hospital.

Admittedly, she was disappointed to see him concentrating on counting out change and not even watching to see if she'd taken the correct road back. Which she had, but it would have been nice to see him return a glance with a little bit of concern when she'd looked back at—

Shanna stopped in midthought, blinked. Automatically switched into doctor mode. Sucked in a deep breath and spun round, then covered the fifty or so yards back to the restaurant before the server had collapsed all the way into Ben's arms. "Symptoms?" she shouted at him over the gasps of the crowd.

He was holding her, half suspended in the air, lowering her gently to the plank floor by the time Shanna literally hurdled over the stone wall surrounding the restaurant's outdoor tables and was at his side. Ben went to his knees with the girl, starting his first assessment of her. "Fever," he said as several patrons came running over to watch, tightening into a narrow circle around Ben and Shanna. "Pale. Shallow respirations. Clammy. Shanna, could you get these people to move back?" he yelled to her over the din.

Without a moment's hesitation she stood and took command of the crowd. *"Por favor. Todos retroceden. Somos médicos. Debemos alojarnos para revisar a esta chica. Por favor, retroceda."* With her words she stepped into the crowd, literally spreading her arms and forcing them back, farther and farther, until the restaurant owner, Señor Raul Varga appeared, and asked everyone standing around outside to, please, go back into the restaurant and have a *yerba maté* or a *licuado* courtesy of the restaurant.

"Thank you," Shanna said, on her way back to help Ben.

"Will she be okay?" Varga asked. "She's my daughter. Graciela."

"You daughter…" Shanna mused. Then asked immediately, "Has she been sick lately? Doing anything different from what she normally does? *Anything* out of the ordinary?"

He shook his head. "Nothing that I can remember, except she's been complaining she's tired. My wife usually knows these things better than I do, but she's away, taking care of her mother. And I think my daughter is doing this for attention because she has to take over some of her mother's duties for a while and she doesn't like it."

Not likely, Shanna thought. Not with Ben down on the floor with the girl, doing a frantic check.

"But other than tired, have you noticed anything else about Graciela?" Varga was not a wealth of information, and she understood he was frustrated with a situation he didn't know how to control—a teenage daughter—but she had to keep pressing him. "Think about it. Was there something you wouldn't normally pay any attention to?"

He frowned. Rubbed his forehead. "Maybe. It was a nosebleed. Is this bad? Is she really sick?"

"When was that?" Shanna asked anxiously. "The nosebleed. When was it?"

"A few days ago. Then she was sick to her stomach. Vomiting a little. But I think it was on purpose." The increasing worry on his face said just the opposite.

"Anything else?"

"Let me think, please." Varga shook his head, shut his eyes.

"Has she had a headache?"

He nodded. "Yes! A little, maybe. She's been working hard, complaining because she wants to do other things. But I thought she was playing sick so she could go to Buenos Aires with her friends. They had a trip planned to visit the *Museo de Arte Latinoamericano,* and I wouldn't let her go because I needed help here. So I thought she was being…how do you say, *petulante?*"

"Petulant," Shanna said, realizing this was far more than a case of a teenage girl trying to get her own way. "Look, I'm pretty sure Dr. Robinson's going to want Graciela in the hospital, so if you have a vehicle…"

"A truck," Varga said, full concern finally registering on his face.

"Good. Go bring it to the front of the restaurant. And let me tell Dr. Robinson we'll be ready to go in a few minutes." After she told him what she suspected.

"My Graciela is that sick?"

"I think she is." She gave him a reassuring squeeze on his arm. Poor man had thought he was dealing with a contentious teenager, not a very sick one. "But we'll know more once we get her up to Caridad."

"Slow pulse," Ben said, when Shanna returned to him and knelt down. "Respirations still labored but not getting worse. And without a thermometer I'm guessing three or four degrees of fever."

"Specifically, *yellow* fever," Shanna said.

Rather than questioning her, Ben looked over at her, frowning. "How so?"

"History of bloody nose the past few days, nausea, headache…with a slow pulse and a fever… Am I wrong?" she asked, wondering what his intent stare was about. "Is that why you're frowning at me?"

"That's a frown of admiration," he said, "because I think you're spot on."

"But you already knew, didn't you?"

"Saw her having some back spasms earlier, so I was guessing. Nothing confirmed, though."

"Well, I may be late with the diagnosis, but I've got a truck ready to take her to the hospital. Unless you beat me to that, too."

He smiled. "It was a brilliant catch, Shanna, for someone who's never practiced in the jungle before. You, um…you haven't practiced in the jungle before, have you?"

A brilliant catch? That pleased her, actually. She'd had compliments before. Lots of them, some because she'd done something good and more than a fair share of kiss-up compliments because she was a Brooks and someone wanted something from her, or her family. But Ben's praise was genuine, and it felt good. "No, I haven't. Just imagine what I could do if had," she said just as Varga rolled up outside in his truck.

Forty minutes later, Graciela Varga, who was floating in and out of consciousness, was isolated in a small hospital room as far away from the rest of the patient rooms as possible, one of three Ben used as his intensive care. He was overseeing the administration of IV fluids when Shanna entered the room. "What's next?" she asked him. Except for the last few minutes, trying to explain to Graciela's mother, by phone, what was going on with her daughter, and at the same time trying to console an unconsolable Raul Varga, she hadn't been more than a few feet away from Ben since they'd admitted the girl.

"Wait and see. Since there's no treatment, we treat her symptoms, keep her fever down, keep her hydrated and make sure she doesn't get a urinary infection or pneumonia."

"What about the village? If we've got one case, aren't we at risk here for more?"

"In the two years I've been here, I've made sure as many people as were willing were vaccinated. So I'm not expecting an outbreak. Maybe some isolated cases, but nothing we can't deal with." He looked point blank at her. "Have you been vaccinated?" he asked.

Her reply, "It left a tiny pinprick scar. Want to see where?"

He didn't answer, of course. Instead, he handed her the chart. "She's yours. If you have any questions about what to do, ask."

"And I'll bet you're off to do a midnight run of yellow fever vaccinations. Right?"

"Am I that transparent?"

"Of course you are," she quipped, then headed off to the medicine room to see what kinds of antibiotics they had in large supply, just in case. The thing was, Ben wasn't really transparent in any sense of the word. In fact, if ever she'd known anyone who'd be difficult to see through, it would be him. He held tight to every little nuance of himself, didn't let anything go without a fight.

The reason she'd known he'd go back to the village to administer vaccinations was because that was the little piece of him he'd let her see. He was a humanitarian, so human-centered that the needs of the village came first. "And tomorrow you'll sleep," she murmured.

Ben was someone to admire in a world where people like him usually went unnoticed. In Ben's case, unnoticed by choice. Another of his off-

limits subjects, she guessed as she started counting the various vials and pill bottles of penicillin.

"So, why am I here?" she mused as she shifted
her count to the doxycycline. "To be like Ben."
The thing was, she wasn't seeing Ben in the same
light she had when she'd come here. And that was
where it got complicated, because what Ben dis-
played on the outside and who he was on the inside weren't anywhere close to being the same.

And the more she watched him the more she
wondered if she might not be patterning herself
after the wrong perception of Ben Robinson. Because the man coming into view wasn't the person she wanted to be but one she might want to…
have. Yes, that was definitely complicated.

"Which is why you need to go south and stay
there with Jack for a little while," Ben argued
with Amanda.

"I've been vaccinated, and I'm not going to
catch anything."

"And I found three more mild cases of yellow
fever last night." He pointed to her rounded belly.
"Do I have to remind you…?"

"That I'm pregnant? No, Ben. You don't. And
I'm being cautious."

"Not cautious enough. And Jack agrees with me on this. You shouldn't be here until we know if these are just isolated cases or a full-blown outbreak. And he does miss you. So does your son."

"If I leave, you'll be short-handed," she argued

He glanced at Shanna, hoping for some support. In these arguments with his sister he never won. Never had. Probably never would. And she was correct in that she wasn't at risk of catching yellow fever. Still, there were always the oddball cases. "Just go. Make me feel better. For once, let me win an argument."

"And I can cover for you," Shanna volunteered. They were sitting in the cramped lounge. Ben was all rigid on the wooden chair in the corner, Amanda was sitting on the two-seat sofa, with her feet up, and Shanna was sitting cross-legged on top of the table, a pseudo-meditative position, not that she was meditating there, more that it was the only place to sit comfortably with the other spots occupied. And she was tired to the bone. Run ragged these past twenty-four hours. Hoping for an adrenalin push to get her through the next several.

"Starting now. Which means..." She swept her

hands in a shooing motion. "Go. Get out of here. We're fine."

"That's not the point," Amanda said, looking first at Shanna then at Ben. "My brother overreacts."

"And my brothers overachieve," Shanna countered. "They're not going to change. Doubt Ben will, either."

"So you're taking his side?"

"No sides to take. You've got a lovely husband and son out there who'd probably be overjoyed to have you spring an unexpected trip on them. Take it from someone whose ex-husband wasn't so lovely—join them. Enjoy what you've got. Let Ben quit worrying about you."

"You have an ex-husband?" Ben asked, totally flummoxed by her casual announcement. Somehow he'd never pictured her married. Or involved. Or anything. Stupid of him, really. Why wouldn't she have an ex-husband/or a current one, for that matter? Even an involvement. Shanna was sensational. Could have her pick of men. "Would he be off limits?"

Shanna shook her head. "Not off limits. Just not worthy of wasting good breath on. He happened at a time when I wanted a pat on the head from my family. As it turned out, he wanted my family's name. Daddy shoved him in my direction, not sure what came after that, but two months later we were married. I like to think of it as a marriage of inconvenience, because nothing worked out with it, except he got himself into my family, even took the family name. The only good thing that came of it was the divorce."

"He actually took your name?" Ben asked.

"In a hyphenated version. Dr. William Henry Morrison *hyphen* Brooks. I wanted to add the initials BD after that, for Big Deal, because that's what he thought he was. But he didn't think that was funny."

It was, though. And Ben laughed out loud at the mental image he was forming of Dr. William Henry Morrison *hyphen* Brooks, Big Deal. "So *you* divorced him, not the other way around?"

"I divorced him, and I would have done it twice if I could have. Although, as a parting gift, I let him keep my name, and my family let him keep his position at Brooks. In deference to my ex, he's a good doctor, brilliant neurosurgeon, and he's turned himself into the third son my father never had. No bitter feelings, though. William got what he wanted and I got my freedom back before we did anything like that." She pointed to Amanda's belly. "Speaking of which, do you need helping packing your bag, Amanda?"

"You're not the most subtle person I've ever met," Amanda replied, pushing herself up off the two-seat couch. "And while I appreciate the offer, I'm not going to take much with me. Just enough clothes for a few days. Oh, and, Ben…" she turned a pointed stare on her brother "…since you're forcing this on me, I'm going to raid supplies so I can take some things down to the orphanage. If there's anything you don't want me taking, let me know."

"I already have a couple of boxes packed for Richard out on the porch, ready to go." He glanced at Shanna to explain. "An orphanage we help support. Richard Hathaway operates on meager supplies—more meager than we do—and we try to help him out where we can."

"When you don't have enough yourself?" Shanna asked.

"That's why I named the hospital Caridad—charity. We do what we can when we're able. Not everybody's fortunate but everybody's deserving."

"What you're deserving of, Ben," she said, uncrossing her legs and scooting herself to the edge of the table, "is some sleep. We've got two other doctors up and working right now and we can handle anything that comes in. So don't argue with me, okay? You look tired. Go take a nap, and I'll come and get you if we need you. Maybe fix you some of that yerba maté tea after you get up, even though I didn't lose the bet."

"You know me. Yerba maté is hard to resist." So was Shanna. And as much as he hated admitting it, he *was* feeling tired, more so than usual. Maybe a nice, cool shower then a couple hours' sleep would do him some good. "Okay, I'm going. No argument," he said, also standing. On his way out the door he gave his sister a squeeze on the arm. "Tell Jack to tie you up, if that's what it takes."

"I love you, too," Amanda replied, laughing. She turned to Shanna. "And you get to tie him up, if that's what you have to do."

"I heard that," Ben shouted from down the hall.

"I meant you to," Amanda shouted back.

"My brothers and I were never like that," Shanna said.

"You mean close?"

"Close, friendly. My whole family's demeanor is…I guess the best way to describe it is that we keep ourselves emotionally separated. I mean, there's love, don't get me wrong, but we don't show it. Don't acknowledge it. Most of the time we just have our own agendas."

"Even when you were children?"

"Especially when we were children. Because we were in training then."

"Training for what?"

"To be who we were supposed to be—a Brooks," Shanna said with a wistful smile. "You're lucky to have a brother like Ben. Lucky to be so close."

"I know," Amanda said as she exited the room.

A cool shower and a nap—not quite as good as Tuscany, but he'd take it. At thirty-six, he wasn't exactly old but the muscles were tightening up on him a little more often these days. The body wearing down a little faster. Oh, he could still keep up the pace. Keeping it with a nap thrown in made it easier, though. Especially on days like today where he just felt beat.

With a weary sigh Ben stripped himself bare in his room then trudged to the bath, taking care not to look in the floor-length mirror as he passed it by. Why torture himself? Truth was, he'd thought about having it removed and keeping only the shaving mirror in the bathroom. That would have been another cop-out, though, and in a life filled with too many cop-outs with bad results already, this one just didn't measure up.

So he simply plodded on by, headed straight to the shower and stepped in, hoping the cold spray would chill some sense into him. Because, damn, he had Shanna on his mind. Couldn't get her out of it. Couldn't quit thinking about her married, or not married, or sitting across the table from him all bundled up until only her eyes were showing.

She'd hit him hard, which was why he turned on the water full spray and let its moderately cool pelting sting his skin. He didn't need to be thinking about her, not in the way he was trying to avoid. Even now, in not thinking about her, he was thinking about her so intently he felt the ache start in his groin. Then the throb. Before it went further, he punched the water faucets off, grabbed a towel and slammed the shower door back so hard it broke off its hinges. Not that it mattered, because they were his hinges, weren't they? So he could break them any damn way he wanted.

Although to break them because he was thinking of Shanna—that wasn't acceptable. Nothing about the crazy way he felt when he was near her was acceptable. So, after a hasty hit with the razor to his stubble, and a comb through his hair, he threw on a pair of cotton boxers and a T-shirt and tumbled into bed, face first, already worrying that he wouldn't be able to take advantage of the next couple of hours.

Too often he didn't sleep even when he had the time off, like he did right now, because his head was filled with so many things—the hospital, his mother, who was fading away to old-age illnesses, his sister, a long life of emptiness ahead of him. Mind-sucks was what he called them. A litany of stresses meant to keep him awake.

Right now, though, it wasn't a mind-suck that wouldn't let him close his eyes. It was Shanna. And the instant she popped into his mind, that ache in his groin wasn't far behind. "Damn," he muttered, turning over and staring up at the ceiling, starting to count the revolutions of the overhead fan.

He was somewhere near a thousand revolutions when the ache subsided.

He was closer to two thousand when he finally dozed off.

Yerba maté tea. Herbal, grassy taste. Chock full of caffeine. And to her tongue peculiarly bitter. But Ben liked it. Lived on it, as she hardly ever saw him without a mug of it in his hand. It did smell lovely steeping, but sometimes the senses were deceptive. Her senses about Ben? Not deceptive as much as confused.

What she wanted to see in him was definitely there, but the whole picture was different. What she'd thought was a healthy wall of dispassion wasn't dispassion at all. He drove himself harder to take care of his patients than anyone she'd ever known. Like spending an entire night knocking on doors to look for people who needed vaccinations. Or pacing the hospital's halls hour upon hour, simply looking in on patients, attending to the little things like drinks of water and cool compresses.

Last night, or more precisely the small hours of the morning, she'd peeked into the children's ward only to find him sitting in a rocking chair, rocking a toddler to sleep, needing sleep himself as much as the restless toddler did. There was no dispassion in that. Yet the message he flashed clearly when anybody looked was, *Keep away.*

"So, who are you, Ben?" she asked as she placed the teapot on a tray and headed out the kitchen door with it.

A minute later, standing outside Ben's door, she was trying to figure out the answer to her question and waiting for him to respond to her first knock. Neither thing happened, so she shoved the question aside and knocked again, only to be met with no response. "Ben," she finally called through the door. "Your yerba maté tea awaits. Open up."

Again, nothing. Her third attempt came with a twist of the knob, and she found the door unlocked. Shoving it open a crack, she didn't enter, but called, "Ben, it's time to wake up and smell the tea. You in there?"

Only silence greeted her. A good hip shove to the door opened it, and she stepped inside. Saw him stretched out in bed. Long, muscular. The sight of him nearly took her breath away, he was so gorgeous, just lying there in sleeping innocence. She couldn't help staring for a moment. Admiring the physical aspect of him. Definitely a man who brought some kind of response to the surface, and it was a whole lot more than tingles and goose bumps. Clearing her throat, trying to avert her thoughts as well as her eyes, she began, "I brought you some—"

But Ben finished her sentence and ended her mood when he lurched up in the bed, and bellowed, "What the hell are you doing in here? Get out, Shanna!"

His voice and demeanor startled her so badly she stepped backward, tripped and dropped her tea on the floor, breaking the teapot and cup and splashing the yerba maté all over the wall and floor in the entryway. In her scurry to sidestep the mess, she didn't see Ben jump from the bed and practically sprint across the room. But she heard the bathroom door slam, and the only thing she could think was that he must have been sleeping so soundly she'd startled him out of a dream.

"I'm sorry," she called to him. A frantic look for rags or a towel to clean up the mess netted nothing. "I thought you'd like some tea before you went back on duty…"

"I'll clean it up," he shouted, his voice flat, inhospitable. "Just leave me alone and shut the door on your way out. And in the future, when I want tea, I'll take care of that on my own."

She'd made an effort, and even though it had turned out badly, that was all she got from him? *Shut the door on your way out?* She wasn't angry. More like hurt. Okay, so maybe she'd overstepped the mark, and maybe she shouldn't have barged into his room because he was, after all, a very private person. But, darn, she hadn't expected this reaction. Hadn't deserved it either, in her opinion. Well, so much for trying to be nice. "Fine," she snapped. "I'll shut your door."

She really wanted to slam it, but she didn't. Instead, she shut it quietly, listened to the hollow click, then went across the hall to her own room and listened to her own hollow click. It really wasn't right, feeling so dejected about what had just happened, but she did. And for the next ten minutes she sat on the edge of her bed, wondering why she'd bothered in the first place.

Was she simply trying to get Ben to like or notice her, the way she'd spent a lifetime trying for those very same things with her family? Or were her feelings for Ben turning into something she'd never counted on?

Neither would come with a happy ending because they were hinged on something in Ben that wouldn't be budged. Yet here she was, trying to budge him anyway, when she was the one who needed budging.

For the first time it occurred to her that Ben wasn't going to be able to teach her what she wanted to be taught. Which meant there was no reason to stay.

Except she wanted to. And that was the thought that sent her running for the shower, to wash off the tea and, hopefully, wash away some of the confusion. Because she really, truly didn't want to leave here, and the only reason that could be happening was that she was falling for someone who would never return her feelings. And that was what had got her here in the first place—her feelings.

CHAPTER SIX

HE REALLY wanted to lob the damned medical reference book at the wall. In fact, it was in his grip, ready to go, and the only thing stopping him was that someone out in the hall would hear it and come running. Then there would be questions, and he'd have to make up answers because he wasn't about to tell anybody that he'd spent the last two hours fretting over things he couldn't control. So what if she'd seen him...all of him? Did it make any difference? They weren't involved, weren't going to get involved. And she was a doctor after all. She'd seen scars. Even ones as bad as his.

But the look on her face...had he imagined it there? Or really seen it? Because it was no different than the look on Nancy's face that day he'd trusted her enough to let his guard down. Nancy had gasped. So had Shanna. And Nancy had turned away. Shanna? He didn't know what she'd done because she had been so involved in reacting to her spilled tea that he'd seized that opportunity to run for his clothes.

He shouldn't have yelled at her, though. After all, he was the one who'd invited her to stay in his cottage. Sooner or later she'd have noticed more than the few scars that showed on his neck. She would have seen those on his arm, shoulder, chest, down his belly to his hip, and halfway down his leg. It's who he was. *What* he was. And Shanna was perceptive. She'd already asked. Already started connecting the proverbial dots. Alcohol in his past, scars... And a lot more hideous dots to connect.

Tension running the length of his arm, Ben gripped the medical reference book so tight his knuckles turned white, then he stared at the book, willing it back to its spot on the shelf lest his frustration got the better of him. Normally, these things didn't matter. He resigned himself to what he could and couldn't have, and got on with life. But Shanna...why the hell was she stirring up these longings after he'd put them to rest? After he'd convinced himself it didn't matter anymore? And there were so many regrets attached to those longings. Damn, he had a list of them.

Ben looked at the book in his hand again, started

to relax his grip then without thought or further provocation hurled it at the wall, knocking his medical diploma to the floor, along with the photos of his parents. It hit so hard it actually dented the wall. Didn't break through so much as dimple it. But it was a dimple heard up and down the hall outside because immediately someone knocked on the door. Then there were shouts. And more knocking.

"I'm fine," he shouted out to them, trying to maintain more control in his voice than he felt. "Just dropped something." More like his self-confidence dropping to the floor, shattering.

"Don't suppose a pot of yerba maté would fix something for you, would it?" one familiar voice rang out.

Naturally, she would be there to hear. Humiliation heaped on his earlier humiliation. Still, just hearing her voice, even though it was locked away on the other side of the door, made him unbend just a little. "But didn't you break my teapot?" he yelled back when he was convinced he could control the sharp cut that wanted to overtake his voice. Normally he wasn't this edgy. Normally he let these things go without acting out. Normally... What the hell was normal, anyway?

"I bought you another one in the village. Actually, I bought two, just in case."

Just go away, he thought. *Please, just go away, Shanna.* Even as he was thinking the words he was on his way to open the door to her. No barriers in place to stop him. "Before you come in, not a word. Okay? I'm just like everybody else. Get angry. That's all it was. Me getting angry." He pointed to the book. "I'm sorry about earlier, too, when you came to my room, and now I'm just..."

"Letting off a little steam."

"A whole lot of steam. Sometimes it builds up."

"I know the feeling. I threw a chair through a plate-glass window once," she said, bending down to pick up his diploma and photos from the shards of broken picture glass. "Meant to do it, too."

In spite of himself, Ben laughed. "I can picture that."

"You can?" she said, looking up at him. "Nobody else in my world could. In fact, they were pretty indignant about the whole thing, about how I'd had the audacity to react."

"React how?"

"In opposition to my family. I was fourteen or fifteen. I had a boyfriend. You know, love of my life and all that. And I wanted to go somewhere with him...don't remember where." She laughed. "Don't even remember his name. But my father refused to let me go because the Brooks family was going to be hosting some kind of event...we always hosted events. So, true to my teenage nature, I threw a tantrum." She stood and handed the photos and diploma to Ben.

"My tantrums were pretty much overlooked, though, because they were...quiet. No throwing books at the wall and breaking glass. More like a very passive *please let me.* Except that never got heard. Or if they heard me, they ignored it. So this one time I decided to get their attention. Actually, it was the beginning of several times I tried to get their attention. Other stories for other days because this was the beginning of Shanna, the wayward teenager."

"Who threw a chair out the window as her prelude." An image he liked.

"Actually, it was an antique Windsor sidechair worth about fifteen thousand dollars. Broke it to pieces. Dozens of pieces. No way to have it restored."

The smile on his face widened. "But did you feel better afterward?"

"Did you feel better after you threw the book?" she countered.

"A little," he admitted.

"A lot," she admitted. "Probably because that one act got me the first honest reaction I'd ever seen from my father. He was really...mad. Yelled at me. Stood over me when I cleaned up the broken glass. Took away all the privileges a girl that age has. *For a month!*"

"You liked that?"

"What I liked was knowing that I had the ability to make my father respond."

"Which you used over and over?"

She shrugged. "Like I said. Stories for another day."

"So, overall, how did that turn out for you?"

"Don't know yet. Time will tell, I suppose, because I'm still wayward, or willful, or whatever you want to call it. Look, I'm going to run down the hall and grab a broom and dustpan to get the glass cleaned up. You get to clean it up, though."

"After which you're going to suspend my privileges for a month?"

"Only if you want them suspended, Ben."

She was like a magnet. He couldn't help himself. As much as he didn't want to be drawn, he was. "Guess that depends on what's being suspended, doesn't it? Like my common sense," he said. "I'm really sorry about earlier, Shanna. You caught me…off guard."

"We all have our moments. Don't worry about it."

"But you didn't deserve one of *my* moments. They're…"

"Intense?"

"That's putting it mildly." Only there was nothing mild about his reactions. Most of the time he held them back, but with Shanna…seeing him figuratively bare came close to seeing the worst of part him, the part that still festered. And he couldn't deal with her seeing that. Just couldn't deal with it.

"You've got a way to go to equal some of mine, Ben." She smiled. "Like I said, we all have our moments, and a couple of mine really stand out."

"That bad?" he asked.

She laughed. "Worse." Spinning, she headed off in the direction of the supply closet, and while he was tempted to step out the door and watch her when she turned and scurried down the hall, he didn't. An old-fashioned page over the loud-speaker called him to Pediatrics, where Nurse

Teresa Vera stopped him just short of entering the ward. "We've just readmitted Maritza Costa. She was complaining of another cold, had a little congestion in both lungs. Dr. Francis saw her in Emergency a little while ago and decided to have her stay."

Maritza Costa, a beautiful little girl with a bad heart. He didn't have the facilities here yet to treat her the way she needed, and her parents didn't want to send her to another hospital. Truth was, the child needed surgery very badly. Attempts to seal the hole in her heart through a cardiac cath had failed, and now it was a waiting game. Waiting, and a lot of finger-crossing, because Maritza wasn't going to get better without the surgery, and their best hope at present was to pray she didn't get worse. With an extra prayer tossed in that her parents would have a change of heart. No such luck, though. "Any problems other than congestion? Did you run an EKG?"

"EKG showed no significant changes. And no other medical problems except…"

Vera paused, obviously not sure that she should proceed.

"Except what?"

"She hasn't smiled, Doctor. Not once."

In most patients that wouldn't be considered a symptom, but in Maritza it was a huge sign that something else was going on because, no matter what else was happening to the child, Maritza smiled her way through it. It was something everybody at Caridad counted on. "I'll go and take a look, see if I can figure it out."

"I promised her ice cream but she says she's not hungry."

"Well, bring some anyway, and let's see what we can do."

In Pediatrics, Maritza had her own private bed, the one on the end where she could look out the window and watch the main street of the village. "So you're back again?" Ben said, pulling up a chair and sitting down next to her. Right away he saw it—the listlessness in her eyes. All the brightness usually there had drained away.

Maritza nodded but said nothing.

"Maritza, sweetheart, where don't you feel good? Can you tell me if something hurts, or just doesn't feel right?"

She shrugged and looked away. But not out the window. More like, she was staring off into space.

"It's okay if you don't answer me, but I'm going to listen to your chest now. I need to figure out what's making you feel this way." He placed the stethoscope into his ears then leaned over to have a listen to her chest. Definitely congestion. Wheezing bilaterally. "Could you turn over on your left side just a little?" he asked, then listened again when she did. "That's good. So, do you have a sore throat?" he asked. "If you do, I understand why you're not talking. It hurts to talk, doesn't it?"

She nodded.

"Can I have a look at your throat?" he asked, fishing through his pocket for his penlight. "I'm going to put a tongue depressor in your mouth, Maritza, so you may gag a little bit. But it will only take me a few seconds to look." Which was what he did. Quick peek, pink throat. Not flaming red, thank heavens. No fever either, according to her chart. But he still had a nagging suspicion…

"Three ice creams," Shanna said, carrying three bowls to the bedside, one of them so heaped with ice cream it was dripping over the sides. She looked at Maritza and smiled. "He really likes ice cream," she said, perching herself on the edge of the bed, handing Ben's bowl to Ben, setting her bowl aside and scooping out a spoonful for Maritza. "All they had in the kitchen was vanilla, but if you have a favorite flavor, I can look for it next time I'm down in the village."

"Vanilla's good," Maritza whispered, then took the spoon from Shanna, looked at it for a moment and finally lifted it to her lips. Took a tiny bite, winced when she swallowed and tried again.

"Maritza's been with us before," Ben explained, picking up his bowl of ice cream then standing. He ducked out of the cubicle, gave his ice cream to the only other child in the room today, ten-year-old Nayla, admitted with appendicitis and now excited to be the lucky recipient of the largest bowl of ice cream she'd ever seen in her life. "Ventricular septal defect," he said, stepping back over to Maritza's bed.

"Repaired?" she asked.

Maritza shook her head as Ben answered, "No. Not yet."

She addressed the girl. "Have you been to see a dentist lately, Maritza? Someone who looked at your teeth?"

"Yes," she whispered.

"Your parents took you?" Ben questioned, picking up Shanna's bowl of ice cream and simply holding it. Better the ice cream than clenching his fists. But he was angry. Damned angry. He'd specifically told her parents… "Was that when the traveling dentist came through last week?"

Maritza nodded.

He gripped the bowl even tighter. So tight the chill of it, combined with cutting off the blood supply to his fingers, caused a dull ache to set in. "Well, I think maybe I should…" The things he wanted to say to them, and would force himself to hold back, were giving him a headache, especially after he'd specifically given them the list of things Maritza should and should not do. "Should go find some medicine for you. But it's going to be in an IV, Maritza. You remember what that is, don't you?" Poor child. She didn't deserve this.

"Yes," she whispered as she attempted one more bite of the ice cream, then set the bowl aside and slid down into the bed, ready for a nap.

"Good. You sleep for a while," Shanna said gently, pulling the sheet up over the child. "As soon as we get some of the medicine into you, you'll start feeling better."

Maritza nodded as her eyes fluttered shut, and Ben instinctively laid a hand to her forehead. Definitely a fever now. Too hot. Too sick. "Bacterial endocarditis," he said gravely. "And she belongs in a hospital that can treat her heart condition as well as… You know, I specifically told them not to take her to the dentist. He comes through every few months, and Maritza's parents asked me if it would be okay to set up an appointment for her."

"But they didn't listen," Shanna said, sliding off the bed. "Are you okay, Ben?" she asked. "You seem agitated."

"Try angry," he said, walking away from the bed. "Enough to throw more than a book, which I'm not going to do."

Shanna caught up to him and they didn't speak until they were outside the ward. "Why hasn't her ventricular septal defect been corrected?" she finally asked.

"Her parents won't let us send her to one of the hospitals that can perform the surgery. They won't go very far from the village, won't let their daughter go very far."

"But do they know it's a correctable condition? That the longer they postpone it, the more difficult it's going to be?"

"They know all that, but they believe that as long as they bring her here she'll be fine."

"And pretty sick now, with a heart infection." Because bacteria had entered her system through a dental procedure. Common and frustrating. "So, can we send her someplace else now? Because this is going to get tricky."

Ben stopped, leaned against the wall, shut his eyes, trying to mentally will away his headache. "I'll talk to them again, but I'm not holding out a lot of hope. Amanda and I have tried everything we can think of and so far it's falling on deaf ears."

"Or frightened ears," Shanna said sympathetically, immediately connecting to the pain and fear of Maritza's parents. "It's hard to move in a different direction when it scares you to death."

"But they know they can go to the hospital with her if we transfer her." He opened his eyes, straightened up. "You're right, though. I'm sure they're scared to death. But so am I, because we could lose her."

"Look, how about you go and talk to her parents since you know them, and I'll get an IV started in Maritza. Then I'll get some blood cultures going so we'll know what we're dealing with. And, Ben, relax. You're looking as stressed as Maritza looks sick."

"Easier said than done," he said as she walked away. Especially when his stress was about Shanna.

* * *

"Another case of yellow fever admitted." Shanna caught up with Ben in the corridor between their rooms. "And Maritza's stable." It had been a long day and she was ready to be off her feet for a while. "Her fever was elevated this evening, but the antibiotics should kick that pretty quickly."

"And her parents are still refusing to let me send her somewhere else, so nothing's changed with that."

His emotional level over this was much the way hers usually was, and it was interesting to watch because in Ben it didn't look like a weakness, which was the way she characterized it in herself. "Did they ever tell you why they allowed the dental procedure?"

He leaned back against the wall, folded his arms over his chest. Sighed heavily. "It was a free exam. They were trying to be good parents, and they didn't think an exam qualified as a procedure."

Shanna winced. "Scraping one of those dental scalers over my teeth is more than a procedure. It's torture."

"Well, procedure or torture, either way that's what happened. Look, would you like to come in for a drink? Not yerba maté, as I know you don't like that. But I've got some killer fruit juice. Unless you've got something else to do."

"I'd love some killer fruit juice. Can you give me a minute to go..." She had been going to say "slip into something more comfortable," but that certainly had a sexual connotation, which had no application here whatsoever. "Go change my shoes."

"I'll leave my door open. And I promise not to overreact this time."

In the span of a minute Shanna slipped out of her long cargo pants and oversized camp shirt and into a clean pair of shorts, a fresh T-shirt and a pair of sandals. Now she wouldn't look so much like Ben, who also wore long cargo pants and a below-the-elbow camp shirt. Sexy look on him. Dreary on her. On her way across the hall she wondered if he might have slipped into something more comfortable, too, but as she pushed through his door she saw the same old Ben in the same old clothes. Oh, well. So much for wishful thinking. "I see you cleaned up my mess from this afternoon."

"Shall I grovel to you now, tell you how embarrassed I am?"

Laughing, Shanna waved him off as she crossed

the room and sat down at his tiny kitchen table for two. "For what it's worth, I thought you looked... good. Every now and then I enjoy a good look at a guy in his boxers."

"I take it that's not on your off-limit topics."

She shook her head. "A girl appreciates what she appreciates. No reason denying it."

"And your ex?"

"Definitely didn't appreciate him in any capacity. On our wedding night I caught him doodling his new last name on a pad of paper. And that was the high point of our marriage."

"Ouch," Ben said. "All the hopes and dreams of a new bride dashed to pieces in a doodle."

"No hopes, no dreams and definitely no dashing. But that's when I started formulating my divorce plans. It had been a huge mistake, but I didn't realize it until I said 'I do,' and knew I should have said 'I don't.'"

"And you got out fast."

"No, he delayed it. Was afraid he'd have to let go of my family. So it took a while, but in my mind the marriage lasted three months, even though the paperwork said two years."

"Why did you do it in the first place? Were you

really that desperate to get your family's attention?"

"We all have our flaws. Mine just happens to be trying to please a family who won't be pleased by me. They're…hard to deal with sometimes. They thought I should be married, so that's what I did."

"That's rough," he said. "My father was a very demanding man, kept lots of secrets, told lots of lies, but I don't think there was a day of my life that I ever had to fight for his attention. I'm sorry you've had to do that."

"You know what they say about how something that doesn't kill you only makes you stronger." She took a sip of the juice. It was pulpy, thick and cool, sliding down her throat. And it took long enough to slide that she hoped in the span of those few seconds their topic of conversation would switch. Talking about her failure to please her family made her seem weak, and she didn't want Ben to see her that way.

"So, do we talk about the elephant in the room? I know it's one of your off-limit topics but, Ben…I think we should just get it out of the way. You know, over and done with then move on to the next subject."

He looked across the table at her, didn't flinch,

didn't blink. Didn't do anything until he picked up his glass of juice and took a sip. "I was burned," he said, setting the glass back down. "I was fifteen, got a little sloppy in some car repairs I was doing with my dad, and the result is what you see. Some scars."

Said much too casually. "How extensive?" she asked.

"Neck, shoulder..." He shrugged, shook his head. "Not worth talking about."

Because he'd never talked about it? She'd seen him run when caught exposed, she saw the kinds of clothes he wore to cover up. Something told Shanna the real scars weren't what you could see on the surface. "Maybe not, but I'm sticking to my guns."

"About what?" he asked, clearly relieved she wasn't pursuing the matter.

"Men in boxer shorts. I do enjoy a good look every now and then, and you were a good look, scars included. So, on that note..." she scooted the chair back and stood "...thank you for the juice and the company. But now I'm going to grab a couple of hours' sleep then go back over and sit with Maritza for a while." Handing the glass to Ben as she passed him, she swept by then paused halfway between him and the door and turned to face him.

"My family is all about exclusion, Ben. That's what I grew up with, what I got used to. It's not a good way to have your life develop around you and it's not a good way to choose your life. Whatever you've gone through, whatever else you've done, you don't have to be excluded, and you don't have to exclude yourself. You've proved your place in the world and that accounts for a lot more than…scars."

He didn't respond but, then, she hadn't expected him to. No good-night or parting words of support. He was Ben after all. And the more she knew him, the more she cared. Because with Ben there were no perceptions. He was who he was.

"How long?" Shanna yelled down the hall, already assessing her options.

"Less than five minutes," the nurse yelled back. "Her fever spiked, we tried to cool her down with a sponge bath, but when that didn't work, we called you, and in those few minutes she…"

She'd had a febrile seizure. Then her heart had stopped. "And what was her temperature last time you took it?" Resuscitation

"One hundred-five."

"I need epinephrine," she said, sprinting by the nurse who detoured to the medicine room while Shanna shoved though the pediatric ward doors just as Ben came charging in from the opposite direction. At Maritza's bedside one nurse and a volunteer from the village were already fully engaged in resuscitation efforts when Ben grabbed the laryngoscope and an endotracheal tube off the emergency cart and in two blinks had the breathing tube in place.

"I'll bag," the nurse volunteered as Shanna moved in to start chest compressions while Ben readied the defibrillator in the event Maritza's heart didn't resume its rhythm on its own. "I called for epi," she said as he stepped back to ready the defibrillator. "But I'd rather not interrupt the resuscitation to use it if we don't have to."

"Because?" Ben asked.

"Side-effects. At Brooks, we instituted what's being recommended internationally, which is high-quality, rapid CPR with minimal interruptions, including not interrupting to administer medication. I went to a conference in Oslo and researchers there…" She stopped. "Bottom line, keep the CPR going, do the drugs afterward. But you know that, Ben. Didn't you write a response to one of the journal articles on it?"

"You read my response?"

"I read several of your responses," she said, getting ready to step back so Ben could attempt a cardioversion—shock Maritza's heart back into a normal rhythm. Once she saw he was ready, she stopped chest compression for a split second, looked at the heart monitor, saw nothing but the tell-tale squiggly tracing of ventricular fibrillation, where the heart was jiggling but not beating, then moved into place with the paddles. "Back," she cautioned the nurse as she herself stepped away and allowed Ben to come forward and administer the first shock to Maritza's chest.

Everybody in the room held their collective breaths for a fraction of a second, watching the heart tracing on the portable EKG machine continue to waver across the screen. Then, just as Shanna positioned herself to start compressions again, the first blip appeared. Then the second, the third…

"Hold off bagging her," Shanna instructed the nurse as she put a stethoscope to the girl's chest to see what was going on in there. A breath sound, a heartbeat… It was amazing how, after a sputter, Maritza was breathing again, fighting against the breathing tube. Not awake yet but returning to life.

"Welcome back," Ben said to the child. Then he turned to Shanna. "Now we get her transferred. Her parents are going to listen to me or I'll be taking her to *El hospital para la Cirugía Cardiovascular* in Buenos Aires myself."

"We didn't call them," one of the nurses said. "Didn't have time."

Ben looked out the window at Maritza's view of the village, all of it lit up now, casting a yellow glow against the black of the night. "That's fine. I'd rather talk to them at home anyway. Care to take a walk with me?" he asked Shanna, then signaled for Dr. Francis to stay with the girl while they went to make the notification.

"It's easy for you, isn't it?" Shanna asked Ben a little while later as they approached the Costa home. "Taking charge the way you do."

"I've never thought of myself as a take-charge kind of person."

"But you step up when it's necessary and...lead. Make people want to follow. My father and my grandfather, too, actually, are great leaders, but they do it by force. They demand that people follow them, whereas you simply walk quietly and people want to follow."

She twined her arm through his, fully expecting him to shake her off, but he didn't. And for a few moments someone might have mistaken them for lovers out for an evening stroll, they looked so cozy and perfect together. Well suited, Shanna thought, even though she knew better. Her head was in a fantasy world. Ben was being polite, not shaking her off. That was all. For a little while, though, it was nice. And such a simple thing. She liked simple things. Too bad she hadn't known that years ago.

Of course, if she had, she wouldn't have met Ben. And the more she knew about him, and the closer they became, the more she was beginning to see how truly passionate he was. Of course, if she totally convinced herself she'd made a mistake then there was no reason to be here. She'd come to study the way he distanced himself from his patients when, in truth, he didn't. It was himself he distanced himself from. But she wasn't ready to make the full admission because she wasn't ready to leave. So for now she shoved it out of her head.

"Shanna," he said, before he knocked on the

door, "it's been a crazy day from the beginning to the end and—"

"And we survived to face another crazy day tomorrow," she said, letting go of his arm. What was the point of holding on to someone who didn't want to be held?

"Yes, another day. Look, I'm glad you're here. Whatever brought you here, whatever's keeping you here, I'm glad you're here."

"I'm glad I'm here, too. None of this is what I'd expected but, it's good."

"What did you expect?"

She laughed. "In my isolated world I expected Brooks in a miniature version. Maybe with a few jungle creatures thrown in for good measure."

"Well, the jungle creatures I can do, but this isn't Brooks by any stretch of the imagination. In fact, Caridad is the anti-Brooks."

"You can say that again."

He landed his first knocks on the door. Then stepped back, shoulder to shoulder with Shanna. "Like I said, it's nice having you here, Shanna. You make Caridad better, and I hope that in spite of my ups and downs, you'll consider staying for a while because…" He turned to face Shanna, who was already facing him. "Because we're good together, as doctor and doctor."

"Doctor and doctor," she murmured, stepping up to him.

"Nice medical relationship," he murmured.

"Very nice," she practically purred as she looked into his eyes. "Very, very nice."

By the time Maritza's father opened the door to them, they were locked in an embrace, exploring the depths of their very first kiss. A nice kiss, Shanna thought as the yellow porch light flipped on. Nicer than any kiss she'd ever had. But from a man who would regret it the instant it was over.

CHAPTER SEVEN

THE kiss had been yesterday, today was life as normal. But nerve-racking, considering the dozen or so times she'd walked by Ben already, only to be greeted by the most clinical of nods, with nothing else. She had been right. He regretted the kiss. So now what? How did they get back to the place they needed to be in order to keep working together? Or was Ben actually able to turn it off that easily?

So much for a spontaneous moment gone bad. Although she'd enjoyed it. But that was as much time as she had to devote to thinking about it because her day was full. Her yellow-fever patients were all recovering nicely, Maritza was finally where she needed to be and her doctors there were cautiously optimistic about her recovery. Now Shanna had a dozen patients waiting for her in clinic and if she didn't grab a cup of tea for herself now—*not* yerba maté—it might be hours before she got the chance again. So, on her way to clinic, she ducked into the lounge, put a kettle of water on the free-standing electric burner and was starting to look through Caridad's stash of various teas when she heard familiar footsteps behind her. Immediately, she tensed up. But didn't turn around to face him.

"That kiss probably wasn't the most appropriate thing I've ever done, but I'm not going to apologize for it," Ben said, standing in the doorway, keeping his distance.

He was scowling, she imagined. "Do you want me to apologize? Because from the way you've been avoiding me…"

"Not avoiding you. Just trying to figure out how to handle it."

"It was just a kiss, Ben." Simple admission, complicated reaction. That kiss had shaken her to the soul. "People do it all the time."

"I don't."

Of course he didn't. Ben preferred sitting with his face to the wall. Except it hadn't been a wall he'd been facing when he'd initiated the kiss. And make no mistake, he'd been the one to pull her into him. And not so gently. Not roughly, either. More like possessively. Being possessed by Ben… she'd liked it.

She turned to face him. "It reminded me of the night Jimmy Barstow brought me home from a date. He escorted me to the front porch and we had that typically awkward moment most teenagers do, where you're not sure about the kiss. You know, will he, won't he? Should I, shouldn't I? Should I tilt my head? Open my mouth?"

"Did you?" he asked.

"Tilt, yes. Mouth, no. It was my first kiss, by the way." She wrinkled her nose at the memory. "Not good by any stretch of the imagination. But, still, my first. And in a fifteen-year-old's mind, so romantic."

"Let me guess. Until the front porch light came on."

"Not just a light, Ben. It was a floodlight. Lit up the whole front yard and halfway across the street, blinded me and my date. Then there was my father, who'd grown to about ten times his normal size, as I seem to recall. He was standing in the front door, arms folded across his chest, mean frown on his face.

"In one version of the story he's holding a shotgun and in another he's got two growling Rottweilers on leashes, ready to rip through the screen door. Either way, my father posed this huge threat and that's the part of this story that's never changed."

"So, what did he do?" Finally, Ben's scowl melted down to pleasant interest. No smile there but nothing negative, either.

Shanna shook her head. "Nothing. I expected an earthquake, and got…nothing. He opened the door for me, thanked Jimmy for seeing me home safely, and that was that."

"Were you disappointed?"

"Maybe a little. Normally, the people in my life fight against me. I think just that once I wanted someone to fight for me. Anyway…" she turned back round to find her tea "…last night, it was nice. Don't know what it was about, but I hope it doesn't come between us because I enjoy being here, Ben. Like the work, like you…"

"You had your tongue down my throat," he said, in his typical businesslike voice.

Smiling, Shanna grabbed a bag of oolong then turned back to face Ben just as the tea kettle began its spindly pre-whistle. "Consider yourself lucky. I never got that far with Jimmy. And Jimmy never got that far with me, the way *you* did." Just then the kettle erupted into a full whistle, and Shanna was grateful for the distraction because, yes, she'd had her tongue down his throat and, yes, she'd enjoyed it. And, yes, she'd do it again. That was the troubling part. Knowing what she knew about Ben, she'd do it again.

"I don't do this, Shanna."

He entered the room, stepped up behind her, so close behind her she could feel his breath tickle her neck. Then it happened again, tingles and goose bumps. Only this time she shivered. And she couldn't hide it. He was too close, and she could feel him staring hard at her. Turning around now would mean risking another kiss. But today she wasn't into risks because one more risk and things might change drastically. She didn't want them to so she kept her back to him. "But you did," she said, trying not to sound as unsteady as she felt.

"We let it get out of hand once, but it's not going to happen again because I don't get involved in relationships."

"Are you sure?" she asked. "Because yesterday you seemed like a man on the verge."

"I'm always a man on the verge, but I'm also a man who knows when he has to pull back."

"Then you're missing out, Ben." She side-stepped him to prepare her tea. "Because getting involved on some level is what life's supposed to be about. I'd be lost without my involvements. They've made me who I am. Even my bad marriage played a part in shaping me. Every person I've ever met, every patient I've ever known... It's not good, excluding everything you're afraid will get close enough to touch you."

She turned around. "And that's not just about relationships, Ben. It's everything. It's...life."

"Sounds good when you say it, and for you it probably works. Hell, it probably works like that for just about everybody. But I don't have enough in me to be *more* than what this hospital needs. It's my life, Shanna. Everything I am, and there's nothing left over."

"Then that's what you'll be contented with for the rest of your life?"

"That's what I've reconciled myself to for the rest of my life. My choice."

"Too bad, because everybody loses. The people who surround you. You...me. We all lose."

Ben didn't say a word when she picked up her mug of tea and walked away from him. Even, steady footsteps on the corridor floor. Jerky, unsteady heartbeats inside her chest. Because he was watching her. She could feel it. One kiss. One impulsive little kiss with such an enormous ripple effect. Nobody, not even Jimmy Barstow, had ever evoked the uncertainty and excitement in her in a simple kiss the way Ben had. So now what was she going to do about it?

Nothing. He'd made himself perfectly clear. He was married to his work. And as for her, she hadn't thought straight about anything for months. So who was to say she was thinking straight about her feelings for Ben? She liked him. Liked him enough to kiss him, actually. Liked him enough that she hadn't stopped thinking about that kiss.

But was there really something more than that? Or had that kiss merely been a refuge on a very tumultuous journey? Take one step beyond that kiss and that was when the confusion took over.

So, she had to keep reminding herself that Ben was her refuge for a little while, and only a little while, and that was where she needed to keep him. Shove him back to the edges and she'd be fine. Of course, the way *he* wanted to be kept on the edges was going to make that pretty easy.

"No, I'm fine." Talking to her grandfather was like talking to a wall. Nothing got through to the man except what he wanted to hear, which, in this case, wasn't what she was saying. In his defense, he was a great healer, had the best medical instinct she'd ever seen. But the downside to that came with the little girl who had just wanted to crawl up on her grandfather's lap and have him tell her a story.

In her life there had been no laps, no stories. Only a grandfather who would spend an occasional evening explaining a coronary stent or an implantable cardiac defibrillator to a six-year-old little girl who was clutching a plastic model of a human heart rather than a cuddly teddy bear. "I'm in Argentina right now."

She waved to Ben, who was poking his head into his office to see who was tying up his landline. She grinned sheepishly as she held the phone receiver away from her ear, not really keen on listening to the same loud voice booming the same things he'd told her when she'd left home. "Just seeing the sights for now, Grandfather. It's a beautiful country. Great food. Nice people." Like he would be interested in anything outside his world. "Good health care, too."

Okay, maybe she shouldn't have tossed that last bit into the conversation, but giving good health care was what this sojourn was about. Why she'd left medicine, why she hoped to find her way back. Why she was so confused about how to do that.

"It's nonsense, Shanna." Miles Brooks spoke so loudly Ben grimaced from the doorway on the other side of the room. "A waste of time, and I'm not a patient man. We have a medical center to run here, and we can't keep your position open forever while you're off trying to discover yourself, or whatever it is you're off doing."

She regretted Ben had to hear this, but it was his office, and it had the only private landline in the hospital. Since her cell wasn't getting a signal, she didn't have a choice. Though she hadn't expected Ben to fold his arms across his chest, lean against the door frame and simply listen. Which was exactly what he was doing.

"I'm not trying to discover myself, Grandfather," she said, knowing that wasn't entirely true. There was some self-discovery mixed in there. For the most part, though, she knew who she was, so this journey of hers was more about reconciliation. That was the part that got confusing. She still didn't know what she was trying to reconcile herself to—who she was or to who she had to become. "I'm just taking time to see things I've never had time to see before."

"While we continue working to support your whim. It's irresponsible, Shanna. And it's not fair to your family. You have your obligations to this family and to the medical center, and you're beginning to run out of goodwill, as far as most of us are concerned. We gave you your time, didn't have a choice. But your time's running out."

She shut her eyes and tried blanking out the next two minutes because she knew her grandfather's lecture by heart, knew every word of it, knew every inflection in his voice as he reeled out each and every point in detail, all of them telling her why she was such a letdown to her family, why she was such a screw-up in her duties.

It was easy to shut out, though, and it wasn't like this was the first time she'd shut it out. But what wasn't easy to shut out was Ben hearing it. Two uninterrupted minutes of standing and listening to all the things that made her a colossal Brooks failure, and by the time she'd hung up the phone she felt like she'd been put through the wringer, not because of what her grandfather had said but because of what Ben had overheard. And might believe.

"So there you have it," she said, standing up. "My dirty laundry. Every last speck of it."

"He's not a friendly man," Ben commented, still not budging from the doorway. "The day I sat across the desk from him and he pummeled me with questions, I think I would have rather taken a physical beating. So, how are you doing?"

"Pretty much beat up. Used to it, though. My grandfather means well..."

"For the medical center? Or for you?"

"It's all interchangeable. In my family, by the time we're able to walk, we're already beginning to assimilate. And it's not necessarily a bad thing, Ben. I'm not complaining. Wasn't even unhappy. But...we're just not typical, and sometimes I think that typical might be nice."

"You're a good doctor, Shanna. He's anxious to get you back. I can understand that."

"See, that's the thing. He's anxious to get me back because he wants to win. Wants to get his way."

"Or get his granddaughter back."

She thought about that for a moment. It would have been nice to believe there was some sentiment attached to him wanting her to return, but there wasn't. She was, pure and simple, a practical matter. Her grandfather wanted her back on his terms and anything else disrupted his plans.

"What he doesn't like to lose is control. The thing is, Ben, I don't hate him. Don't even dislike him. My grandfather's a great man, he's been responsible for many advances in cardiac medicine. And look at the hospitals and clinics he's built. I'm in awe of him. And proud of him. But…" She shrugged.

"It's tough being the granddaughter of a medical legacy?"

"Something like that." Especially if you were in search of your own medical legacy and beginning to have grave doubts that it's out there. "My entire family is so driven by what they do there's no room for anything else. Fun for my father is lecturing at a medical conference. For my mother it's publishing another article on the latest discovery in cancer treatment…she's an oncologist.

"You know my grandfather, and my grandmother is dean of a nursing school. My great-grandparents are the same. Great-Grandfather founded the Brooks Medical Center, Great-Grandmother started one of the first schools of nursing in that part of the country. That's who the Brooks family is, and they've cloistered me, but not with bad intentions. They kept my brothers and me separated from all the things other kids our ages were doing because the world we live in is a perfect world…for the Brooks family purpose."

"But not for Shanna?"

She shrugged. "It's a safe world. A whole lot safer than anything outside it. And the people in it are happy, Ben. There's never been a time when I've believed anyone in my family isn't happy."

"Which means Shanna is…"

"Trying to find out if I'm really cut from the family cloth. I've got to know myself better before I go back." Not just know herself better but prove herself worthy. She had to change, or everything about her future with Brooks Medical Center would be changed for her. "And in the meantime I'm going to be checking Beatriz Rivas in a few minutes. Her baby's breech, and as she's getting closer to her due date, I want to see what I can do about turning it."

"An ECV?"

"I know there are a lot of various non-medical traditions on how to turn a baby—playing soft music at the pelvic bone so the baby will gravitate toward it, putting ice at the top of the abdomen so the baby will turn away from it. But an external cephalic version is relatively easy, and if it works it saves Beatriz from having a Caesarean section."

"You've done them before?"

Shanna nodded. "And had pretty good luck. It doesn't always work, but in my opinion it's always worth a try. And since you have that nice ultrasound machine..."

"Thanks to my brother-in-law. When he found out Amanda was pregnant, he ordered state-of-the-art everything for obstetrics. Otherwise I might have to sit near the end of the bed, strum my ukelele and hope the baby turns toward my music."

Shanna laughed. "I didn't take you for a ukelele man."

"I'm not. But my mother always thought I had the music in me, which I didn't, and when I was younger she bought me a mighty fine electric guitar and an amp that turns up so loud it would shake the currasows right out of the trees." He smiled. "Large birds. Size of a wild turkey."

"So you're a rock star."

"Hardly. Haven't touched a guitar since I was a kid. Wasn't very good at it when I did."

"Then the currasows are safe. Good for them, too bad for me. I'd have liked to hear you play."

"Trust me. When I was a kid, nobody liked hearing me play, but it didn't matter because I loved it. Loved the way I shattered windows, knocked things off walls…in the neighbor's house across the street."

It was a new way to picture Ben, talking about something he loved other than medicine. Something she hadn't anticipated but really, really liked. Naturally, her mind went wild with the thought— skin-tight jeans, ab-tight T-shirt, ripped, exposing flesh. That was an unexpected jolt of nice she hadn't seen coming, but one a girl could certainly enjoy lingering on for a while.

"What's the smile about?" he asked.

"Thinking about delivering Beatriz's baby," she lied. "She's thirty-seven weeks now, and I'm hoping I'll be here long enough to do the delivery. Want to help me with the ECV?"

Ben finally stepped into the office. "Give me five minutes, okay?"

"Five minutes. And, Ben, about that kiss…" She'd wanted it. No denying that. No telling him that, either. "I didn't come here to get personally involved, if that's worrying you. We made a mistake, it's over. Live and learn."

"Live and learn. And I'm sorry I put you through my usual reaction."

Shanna laughed. "One thing's for sure—you've got it down to a science."

"They say practice makes perfect."

But for Ben practice brought about heartache. She could see it in his eyes, and that sadness cut right through her. Which was precisely what her grandfather had lectured her about—she was too emotional to succeed at Brooks. So far, though, none of that was changing. And for the first time since she'd left she was beginning to wonder if she wanted to go back there. The question was always out there about her grandfather not taking her back, but she'd never thought she might be the one to sever the ties. It was on her mind now.

"And perfection takes practice," she said, still trying to come to terms with how she might be the one to cut herself off from her family, and not the other way around.

"Well, perfect or not, as a friend, do you want to go down to the village with me later on? Maybe have dinner, listen to some music? No off-limits lists involved."

It was really too bad she didn't want to get involved as much as he didn't want to get involved, because Ben would have been the one. Undeniably, unquestionably, the one. Really, too bad. "In what kind of time frame? I'm assuming you have a time limit on that."

He winced then smiled. "Okay, I deserved that."

Biting back her own smile, she arched playful eyebrows at him. "You're right, you did. So, how about we get through the ECV then see what happens afterward?"

"Fair enough."

She nodded then stepped out into the hall. "Five minutes, Ben." Five minutes to collect her wits, because Ben had just asked her out on a date, whether or not that was what he'd intended. And she'd put him off. Of course, if he'd been standing there in rock-star clothes rather than well-worn and faded scrubs... Thing was, in her mind right now he was in well-worn and faded scrubs, and looking as good as he would in rock-star clothes. Causing her breath to catch, her pulse to increase a beat or two.

Just a reaction to something that didn't exist. That was all it was. Nothing.

When he entered the obstetrics procedure room, the patient was on her hands and knees on the floor and Shanna was sitting on a stool, holding an electric toothbrush. This was where most doctors would have stopped whatever was going on, no questions asked, and quickly come up with another plan. But somehow the doctor with the toothbrush looked like she was totally in control of the situation, and if Ben hadn't already put his faith in her, it was clear from the expression on Beatriz Rivas's face that she had all the faith in the world. So he simply slipped in and took his place standing along the wall, watching and waiting for Shanna's next move.

"I had her start the rocking yesterday," she said to him. "I don't like to give anesthesia before the procedure. Don't even like using tocolytic drugs—" meant as a relaxer "—because they can increase the mother's pulse rate as well as the baby's heart rate, and lower the mother's blood pressure, which can put extra strain on her heart. And that's not to mention they can make her jittery, anxious and nauseated and also send her into labor. So I try the more natural approach, and pelvic rocking helps."

"Makes sense. But the toothbrush?"

"Actually, studies have shown that vibroacoustic stimulation can startle the baby into moving away from the woman's spine, which makes him or her more easy to turn. I just happen to like the buzzing sound an electric toothbrush makes. It's gentle, and I've had it work."

"But no ukelele?" he asked, smiling.

"Sorry. Your uke's untried, my toothbrush isn't." Grinning, she held it up, hit the switch, then let it buzz for a second.

"Somehow I don't see this approach being used at Brooks Medical Center. But I could be wrong."

She shook her head. "Not wrong. If any of my family members walked in on this…" Standing, she bent down to help Beatriz up from the floor. "Let's just say that any encounters you've had with my grandfather in the past would have been a walk in the park in comparison. So now…" She gestured for Ben to turn around as she helped Beatriz into an exam gown, but he chose to leave the room instead. Privacy was his own personal issue, which turned it into a priority for his patients. So often in medicine, when all the basic elements were broken down, and all the tests taken, the only thing some patients were left with was their self-respect. It was always his aim to leave that intact as well as add his share to it.

In this case, he was glad for a short reprieve, where he simply went to the desk across the hall and sat down. Too much work was finally beginning to catch up with him. He was a little achy today, with a bit of a headache. Nothing eight or ten uninterrupted hours of sleep wouldn't fix. Except he didn't have eight or ten hours anywhere in his schedule, and the foreseeable future wasn't going to be any different. Two of his doctors had left the day before and no one had come to replace them.

But in a week, he promised himself. When his new staff was on board and oriented to the hospital, when the final verdict that the yellow-fever cases were isolated and not an outbreak, when a couple of his more critical cases had turned the corner—that was when he'd take his eight or ten hours. Shut his eyes, hopefully dream of Tuscany…

"Ben," Shanna whispered, practically in his ear. "Wake up. Are you okay?" Asked to the accompaniment of gentle nudging.

A moment passed before he was aware of her standing over him, looking down. The back of her hand was laid across his forehead like she was a mother checking a child for fever.

"Don't know how it was where you went to med school, but where I went we had an actual class on catnapping. Taught us how, when, where to grab them, including standing up, leaning on a wall, napping with eyes open so no one will know you're napping…"

"Napping with a fever?" she asked.

He rolled back in his chair to get away from her. "There's a difference between warm and feverish. I'm warm. Need to take off a layer of clothing to get more comfortable."

"What are you denying, Ben?"

"Nothing."

"You're rundown."

"And I'm entitled to be rundown."

"But you got back off a holiday not so long ago."

"More rundown from that than from work."

"It's true what they say, isn't it?" she asked, spinning away from him. "That doctors make the worst patients."

"That would assume I'm a patient. I'm not." He stood, followed her to the exam-room door. "Look, I appreciate your concern, Shanna, but I'm not sick. I'll admit I'm tired, I'll admit I wouldn't mind getting a good night's sleep. That's as far as it goes."

"You're sure?" she asked, before she pushed open the door. "Because I can handle more if you need a day or two off to recover. Or even a night off to sleep. Like tonight. Skip the night on the town so you can sleep."

She spun to face him. Then simply stared. Looked deep into his eyes for so long he wasn't sure if she was assessing him for something or trying to discern a lie the way his mother used to do—that long, hard stare, followed by, "Benny, I know you're not telling me the truth." Only thing was, he wasn't lying about anything. He wasn't sick. Left to the scrutiny of an overly compassionate doctor, that might be the way it looked. But he knew his body…the good and the bad of it. Right now, he was tired. That was all.

Shanna cared. And she worried about him. Worried too much. It was a nice feeling, having someone worry about him outside his mandatory worriers—his mom, his sister and even to some extent his brother-in-law. Nothing he was going to get used to, though. Because Shanna was just passing through, like it or not.

Today, he didn't like it.

CHAPTER EIGHT

"So, where do we begin?" he asked Shanna, deferring completely to her knowledge in carrying out the external cephalic version.

Shanna glanced at him, studied him only the way Shanna could—a hard, through-to-the-bone stare like she was seeing more than he wanted anyone to. Like she was trying to find the soul he fought to keep shrouded. Finally, she nodded.

"I'd like you to monitor the baby's heatbeat, Dr. Robinson, as well as Beatriz's vital signs. Her baseline is already charted, so I think we're good to go."

Smiling at her patient, she exuded confidence and caring. It was written all over her, everything she was, and everything that made her a good doctor. Ben liked the way she cared, the way she got involved. Doctors with that level of passion were hard to find, especially coming from the kind of institution Brooks Medical Center was, and he could understand why her family wanted

her back. She was rare in the profession. Someone to admire for her compassion. "Good with
that," he said.

"So, are you ready to get this baby turned over?"

"*Sí,* Doc Shanna," Beatriz responded.

First, she gave Ben a smile, then she turned her
attention back to her patient. "Okay, first, relax.
You may feel a little discomfort, but you've already had two other babies and this isn't anything
compared to that." Handing Beatriz the toothbrush, she instructed her to simply hold it near
the baby's head, then she examined the woman's
belly until she found the baby's exact placement.

Glancing at Ben, she said, "Normally this is
where I might do an ultrasound to determine the
positioning, but baby Rivas has taken a mighty
strong position against Beatriz's pelvis—his or
her bottom is deeply seated there—so I'm going to
tilt the head of the table down to help baby move
away from there. Except..." she winked at him
"...this table doesn't tilt, so guess what?"

He chuckled. "I'm going to make it tilt. Probably
with a couple of nice big medical texts that work
better to prop up a table than hit a wall."

Two minutes later, Ben was positioning them
under the table legs, making a mental note to go

looking for better exam tables whenever he had the chance. He was welcome to scrounge used equipment in any number of hospitals throughout Argentina. In fact, that was how he'd started Caridad—with scrounged equipment from other hospitals. For now the medical texts were much better suited under the table than against the wall, and Shanna was busy manipulating Beatriz's belly, turning the baby like it was something she did every day.

Watching her, feeling his admiration for her continue to spiral upward, he saw the good rapport she found with her patient. Saw the ease, the caring. Especially saw the way Shanna kept Beatriz smiling with her lighthearted chat about baby names, even though without painkillers the procedure could be excruciating, and probably was. All of it was amazing to watch, every facet of Shanna's bedside manner, every nuance of her skill.

"Okay, now. Just think of this as a tummy massage with a little extra pressure," Shanna said while she oiled up Beatriz's belly then began in earnest the kneading that would turn the baby round, placing her left hand where the baby's head was positioned and the right at the baby's bottom. "You're definitely going to feel some pressure and discomfort, so let me know if the pain gets too bad because we can stop, and I'll give you something to ease it."

"Vital signs holding nicely," Ben said, feeling almost superfluous in the room now as Shanna had everything so much under control.

She smiled at him. "Well, up on this end I'm being kicked. Someone's really fighting me on this move. And from the force of the kick I'm betting we may have a future soccer star here." She leaned a bit more into Beatriz and alternately pushed then rolled the baby to a head-down position for a moment, pausing to slide the ultrasound probe over Beatriz in order to view the positioning. "Not bad," she murmured, twisting back so Ben could have a look.

"He's going to turn right back round, though, isn't he?" Ben asked. "Once you get him fully positioned."

"The stubborn ones usually do. Unless we hold them down for a while. You know, win the battle of endurance." She glanced up at him but didn't smile. Instead her expression was thoughtful, serious. "And that's a battle I always win, Ben. Against stubbornness, against anything else that gets in the way of what I need to do."

Was that a warning to him? "Your point being?"

"For future reference, that's all. You're pale, your eyes have dark circles under them and either you're going to take care of it or I will. Because you need to rest."

"Is it a boy?" Beatriz asked, totally oblivious to the subtext going on around her.

Returning her attention to her patient, softness came back to Shanna's expression. "Yes, I believe it is. And he's a big one. Looks ready for that soccer ball," she answered. "See, to the left? That's his head. And to the right, that's his..." Grinning, she moved back into position. "Definitely a boy, Beatriz. No doubt about it. Did you want a boy?"

Beatriz smiled contentedly. "We have two daughters. A son will be nice this time."

"So, boys' names..." Shanna said, pushing harder on Beatriz's upper abdomen as the baby finally started to co-operate and slide into place. "Esteban, Gerado, Miguel..." Sucking in a deep breath, she bit her bottom lip and pushed even harder. "Rafael, Raoul..." Another solid push, and this time when she sucked in her breath she held it and gave one last final prod to Beatriz's belly. Then let out her breath, smiled and nodded.

"And Nehuen, which means strong, because

your baby is strong enough to give me quite a fight, Beatriz." She nodded Ben over to her side of the table then instructed him where to place his hands. "Dr. Stubborn, meet Baby Stubborn. You two should hit it off well. As for me, my back needs a break so, Ben, will you hold the baby in place for a few minutes so he doesn't reposition himself?"

He laid his hands on Beatriz's belly, let Shanna physically manipulate him to the exact spots she wanted braced, and the feel of her hands with oil on them, sliding over his hands, purposely splaying each of his fingers into position…it was all he could do to focus on the fetal monitor. "Your technique was…I guess the only thing anyone could really say was flawless. When I've seen these done they were always more invasive, stressful. Is this something you learned at Brooks?"

Twisting from side to side to relieve the tightness in her back, she shook her head. "No. We have an outstanding obstetrics department so once my patients are confirmed pregnant, I send them to the experts. Can't say that I've ever actually done the procedure at Brooks. But trying to make the ECV less stressful is something that made sense to me the first time I ever saw one done. I was still a resident, working through my obstetrics rotation. My advisor asked me to assist him in the procedure, which I was glad to do.

'But he was so…rough. Too rough, I thought. Didn't establish rapport with his patient, didn't use oil to make the rub more gentle. A lot of subtle deficiencies, I thought. Then when the baby didn't cooperate he resorted to using more drugs than I care to remember. Drugs were his first line of response and I don't necessarily believe in that if the ECV can be done without them. That's the way I am about everything—the fewer drugs used, the better.

"Anyway, that first time, all I saw was how scared the mother was and how oblivious to her needs the doctor seemed to be. At least, from my perspective, which could have been a little off since it was my first time. The next time he was called out to do an ECV, I asked him if I could try it and I pretty much did just the opposite of everything he'd done and it seemed to work. Could have been a different kind of response from the patient, could have been my ideas were actually good. Don't know. But I liked the result, and continued to use my way throughout the rest of my obstetrics rotation. Haven't done the procedure since then, though."

She twisted a little too hard to the right, winced, grabbed her lower back, then twisted back to the left to straighten out her kink. "Don't get me wrong. My advisor was an excellent doctor and an even better instructor, but somewhere in the mix I think he lost his bedside manner. Watching him, with all his excellent medical skills and his sub-par people skills was when I decided that a doctor's manner in healing is nearly as important as the actual healing."

"Well, however you accomplished it, this baby has surrendered peacefully. He's holding his place just fine." And so was Beatriz, who'd dozed off at the end of a procedure that was often traumatic. Shanna was right, though. The manner was important. And when that manner came from Shanna, it resulted in the smile like the one on Beatriz's face. Like the one he felt in his heart.

Now, even more than before, he wondered what had gone so wrong in her life, or her medical practice, that had caused Shanna to leave one of the most reputable medical institutions anywhere and come to the jungle. Especially one where she was part-owner. Before today, he'd thought it might have been impulse or wanderlust. Or that she was just someone traveling the world in search of herself. All those made sense to him and in so many ways he understood that. Of course, that was coming from the perspective of someone who'd searched for the same thing and walked away empty.

What didn't make sense about Shanna, though, was Shanna herself. Everything she did was well thought-out, nothing came without a precise motivation. And there was nothing about her that was lost. Or, at least, appeared lost on the surface. Which meant there was something much deeper going on with her. Something that made him wonder what would have caused her to pack it in and end up here.

He really wanted to think that the call of the humanitarian cause might have lured her, but he knew better. She had a reason for being *here*. And it was something she wouldn't, or couldn't, divulge to him. So, damn it, what was it? What wasn't she saying?

"Look, I think we're good here," he finally said. "Why don't I go get one of the volunteers to sit with Beatriz for the next couple of hours, and if nothing changes, we can send her home?"

"I could use a break," she admitted. "Go somewhere and try to exercise out the knots."

"Your back aching that bad?"

She nodded. "It comes and goes. Usually just some kinks from an old injury."

"Another one of those Shanna stories? You know, the foibles of youth?"

Nodding, she said, "Big foible." She stepped aside as Consuela Alvarez made her way to the bed and turned to shoo Ben and Shanna on their way. "Big, *big* foible. My family had picked out some kind of surgery for me to pursue, but bad backs and operating tables don't mix."

"I don't see you as a surgeon. Not that you don't have the skill but you like the personal interactions."

"Precisely. But for the Brooks family, family practice is too mundane. Good for someone else but not us."

"Someone else, like me?"

"Obviously, I don't look down my nose at family practice, because it's what I chose. And I think you're a natural for family practice, but I could see you as a surgeon," she said.

He shook his head. "I thought about general surgery for a while. Couldn't see myself tied down to an operating room all day, so I looked for something with some variety. Which, for me, turned out to be what I'm doing. It's good, too, because I like being someplace where the expectations are different."

"You mean expectations of you?"

"No, not of me. But of medicine in general. The people here want to keep it simple. Pure. Maybe fundamental. They're happy to get penicillin, yet during my residency when I prescribed it for a patient I was told it was outdated, that there were better antibiotics, to at least prescribe one of the updated penicillins. Yet, plain, old-fashioned penicillin's a perfectly good drug that works, and it's a lot less costly than any other antibiotic on the market.

"Your ECV's another example. You tried the simple thing first, and it worked. So I guess what's maybe the most important thing to me is that I like the expectation that medicine can still be pure. Or fundamental. And that's not my patients' expectations. It's mine."

"Then you're a country GP at heart, aren't you?"

"And proud of it. The bigger medicine gets, the more impersonal it becomes. But when someone is sick and needs a doctor, they still want to feel like their doctor cares in something other than a corporate-detached kind of way. So long live the country GP, because that's where the true personal medicine is still being practiced."

"The country GP who has found himself happy in a jungle village. There's something quixotic in that, Ben Robinson. I envy you your choice. And your dream."

An expression crossed her face, one that was sad, full of melancholia, and that was when he knew, when he finally could see her conflict. Somehow Shanna was caught between two medical ideals, trying to figure out which one she wanted. That was probably a simplified version of it, but he'd bet his best stethoscope that was where it had all begun for her. "For me, it was a simple choice. I tried it on, it felt right. So I adapted it to fit me."

She smiled. "Well, I think the good thing is that your kind of medicine still exists to give medicine as a whole that more rounded, compassionate edge."

"Until it gets shoved so far back nobody can find it. It's already happening in a lot of places. The United States... Express the sentiment of being a country GP to your colleagues and they look at you like you're crazy. Make a house call? No one does it anymore. Go back to simpler prescriptions? Some pharmacies don't even stock them."

"But the country GP found his country, and his practice, didn't he? And he's practicing happily-ever-after. Isn't that the way it should be?"

"I don't know, Shanna. You tell me."

That sad, melancholic look passed over her face again. "When I was a girl, still in middle school, I accompanied my father on a lecture tour throughout Europe. He's the medical academic in the family. Anyway, most of the time he stuck to the large cities and universities, but in England he went to visit a former colleague who lived in some little village...I don't remember the name. It was old, coastal, very quaint. Buildings two hundred years old that would have been condemned for old age where I came from but still had a vital purpose in that village.

"And the people...they fished for a living. Worked so hard, and seemed happy doing it. There was actually still a millinery shop, Ben. Someone making hats, of all things. I mean, who makes hats?" Wonderment shone in her eyes. "It was the first time I'd ever seen anything outside my own life and I was in awe. I couldn't believe people lived like these people did.

"Anyway, my father's colleague turned out to be someone with whom he'd associated when he was guest lecturer at Oxford. Professor Augustus Aloysius Copp. He referred to himself as a licentiate in medicine and surgery, and I thought that sounded more important than just about anything I'd ever heard. Turns out he was a very important man in the medical field.

"But here he was in a fishing village, this man with the most impressive academic record, and he was working as a GP after such an illustrious career. Picking up his medical bag, walking out the door of his two-hundred-year-old cottage and making house calls on a regular basis to people who lived in other two-hundred-year-old cottages.

"My father and I tagged along with him one day and I kept wondering why Dr. Copp was doing it. It was hard work, all that walking, and he wasn't so young. All I knew was the medicine I saw in my own life every single day. It was very narrow, the way my life was. But, Ben, this was the first time I became aware that there *was* another way. Dr. Copp was happy, his patients respected him and he loved his patients. It was a simple system that worked and he said it was truly the way he'd always wanted to practice medicine."

"But that kind of a system's not for you."

She shrugged. "Not for me. At least, not in the life I have back at Brooks Medical Center."

"Yet here you are, picking up your medical bag and electric toothbrush and making house calls on a regular basis now. And you're enjoying it, Shanna. It shows all over you. How can you explain that?"

"I don't know. Maybe it's something about knowing how the world needs both Dr. Copp and Dr. Robinson."

"It also needs Dr. Brooks, wherever she decides she wants to be."

"*Whatever* she decides she wants to be," Shanna said, her voice bittersweet.

"You'll figure it out, Shanna. When you want to. But in the meantime..." He stopped at one of the exam rooms, opened the door and gestured Shanna in.

"What's this about?" she asked.

He held up his hands. "Good with aching back. Won't cure anything, but will sure make the aches of the moment feel better."

"Really? You'd do that for me?" Before he had

a chance to answer, she scooted into the room and was already halfway up on the exam table. "Never let it be said I don't take full advantage when something good is presented me. So, do you want my shirt off, Ben?"

He gulped. "Your shirt?"

"For the massage. Would it be easier without my shirt?"

Images of Shanna without her shirt flashed through his mind, exploded in his mind, sky-rocketed all around his mind, and it was all he could do to maintain his doctorly comportment. Bad idea, this massage. Especially when he didn't stand a chance of keeping it professional. At least, not in his mind—damned traitor to his resolves.

"No, leave it on," he said, wishing he didn't have to say that. But better safe than sorry. "I can get at the places I need without it coming off." *Unfortunately.*

"Lower back," she said, settling down. "Above the coccyx, just to the…" She sucked in her breath, held it for a moment as his fingers went, almost instinctively, right to the spot. "Yes," she murmured, hoping it didn't sound like a purr. "Right there."

"So, tell me the story of your back injury. Your

big, *big* foible," he said as his fingers applied the first level of pressure. "And the tattoo. What's that about?"

"Tattoo's about my first real act of rebellion. Actually, the second part of my first real act."

"The foible?"

"Yes, the foible. After the whole window-chair incident, I decided I wanted horseback riding lessons. My parents refused. They didn't have enough time to take me, said it was too danger-ous, kept telling me I had better things to do with my time. Take your pick. There was a counter-argument for every one of my arguments." She laughed.

"I will say, it was the first time they ever put up much of a united front against me. Most of the time they deferred me to the other parent, who de-ferred me back, turning most decisions concern-ing me into a volley between two parents who didn't know what to do with me and didn't want to take the time to find out. In the end, I usually got what I wanted because they got sick of the back and forth."

"Making you a very willful child."

He applied a little extra pressure just offside her tattoo, causing her to gasp, suck in a sharp breath, then let it out judiciously. "You really know where to hurt a girl, don't you?"

"On the back, or in the pride?"

"A little bit of both. But you're right. I was willful. Saw my advantages and took them where I could. Except about the horseback riding. I had no idea what to do against a united front. So I ignored their refusal to allow me to do it and did it anyway. One of my girlfriends had a beautiful chestnut mare boarded at a local stable so I'd go with her after school when she'd go to groom or ride her horse."

"And you rode her horse?"

"Not exactly. You know that part where you said I was willful…" She flinched again. "Are you doing that on purpose? Trying to hurt me?"

"You're tensing up."

Because his fingers on her felt so…good. Perfect. Like they were the fingers that should be massaging her back. "I'm tensing up because talking about my family makes me tense," she lied.

"Actually, you were talking about your friend's horse."

"*My* horse," she corrected. "There was a beautiful gray there for sale, so I bought her."

"You had that kind of money when you were

a kid? Because when I was that age I was doing good to scrape together twenty dollars."

"No, I didn't have that kind of money, but I knew the combination to my dad's safe so I took a little bit at a time, hoping he wouldn't notice it missing, or would think he'd miscounted last time he'd checked. Eventually, I had enough to buy a horse."

He chuckled. "Burglary. Good plan. Where I come from, that'll get you sent off to a juvenile correctional facility."

"Where I come from, too. But that's not what happened. I bought my horse, paid for riding lessons and to have her boarded with that money I was taking, and had a perfectly good secret going for over a year. Then I fell off. Got sloppy saddling my horse, didn't get everything cinched properly and took a mighty hard fall on one of the trails. Fractured my back, not seriously but serious enough that I had to be airlifted to a hospital by helicopter."

"Riding in a helicopter with a broken back usually isn't conducive to being kept secret."

"Especially when the helicopter sets down on my family's own helipad, even though I'd specifically told the pilot to take me to another hospital.

Anyway, they'd radioed ahead, and when they pulled my stretcher out of the chopper, there to greet me were my parents, my grandparents and a few other family members. Imagine a whole platoon of Brooks medical workers standing there with scowls and folded arms... The scowls came only after they'd determined I was okay, by the way. But still..."

"Secret's out."

"In a big way. And I had to give my horse back. Then deal with the consequences of going into my dad's safe and taking the money, which turned into the kind of hospital duty no one ever aspires to."

"Did it involve bedpans?"

She nodded. "And that was one of the more pleasant aspects of my punishment."

He chuckled as he shifted the focus of his massage up a couple of inches. "Something tells me that didn't end the rebellion."

"Hardly. My physical therapist...beautiful man, my first adult crush, actually. Let me rephrase that—my first teenage crush on an adult. I fell in love with his tattoos probably more than I fell in love with him. They represented freedom and self-expression. Anyway, he had these big, muscly arms..."

"Unlike mine."

"You have nice arms, Ben. Small in proportion to Lance's arms, but you work out."

"How can you tell?"

"A girl notices these things, even under long sleeves." She noticed it was his muscles that tensed up this time. Could feel it in his touch, in the way he attacked her muscles, going from firm and gentle to nearly pinching.

"Had to start when I was a kid. Didn't see any reason to stop."

Something to do with his own physical rehab? She wondered about it, wanted to ask, but nothing in Ben made him seem inclined to want to tell her about his scars. So she didn't ask. Instead, she returned to her own conversation, trying to keep it light to make him feel at ease, because maybe if he stayed at ease, he'd talk about himself. She hoped he would, anyway.

"Like me. I didn't see any reason to stop rebelling so I got a tattoo. Thought about something dark and sinister like a skull or a snake. Decided I'd rather go artsy. Since I'd broken my back, I choose the Djed, had it put right over my own backbone. It's Egyptian, by the way. And it's believed that the Djed is a rendering of a human backbone. It represents stability and strength."

"Well, your Djed is artsy. Has a nice sarcasm to it, doesn't it? A particularly explicit message, which I'm sure your parents didn't appreciate the first time they saw it."

"After I had it done I was actually going to keep it hidden, but something about a lower back tattoo and a low-cut swimsuit don't go together. We have a pool, and I was sitting out there one day, reading a book, and my grandmother saw it."

"Let me guess. She made a fuss?"

"That's not even the half of it. By the time the whole Brooks clan got through with me, you'd have thought I'd tattooed it in the middle of my forehead."

He moved his hands up another couple of inches, splayed out his fingers on either side of her spine, and applied a much deeper pressure than he'd been applying. "More bedpan duty?"

"Enough to make me the bedpan queen of the world."

"But you got what you wanted, didn't you?"

"My tattoo?"

"No. Attention. You're a smart woman now so

I'm assuming you were a smart girl then. And smart girls know they will get caught stealing their father's money, and buying a horse, and getting a tattoo. Your crimes, Shanna, were all pretty obvious. Anyone looking would have noticed them, which is why I believe you did what you did. To see if your parents were watching."

She'd never analyzed her rebelliousness that way. To her, the things she'd done as a child had been pranks. Stupid, childhood whims. But cries for attention? "They were busy people," she said, not sure if she should defend them or defend herself.

"Busy people with a child who needed to be noticed."

Which had made her seem so willful. And she had been, but that was a long time ago. Still, what if that was what he thought of her now? What if he believed her turning up here was something done out of sheer, petulant willfulness? Everything she'd told Ben led her to that conclusion, so why wouldn't he be led, as well? "That's why you think I'm here, isn't it? You think I'm still the child who wants to be noticed? That coming to Argentina is just a step or two beyond my tattoo?"

Bolting up on the table, she twisted round to

face him on her way off it. "Tell me, Ben. Is that the conclusion you've drawn? That I'm looking for attention so I came out here into the middle of nowhere hoping somebody notices me? That I'm being...manipulative?"

"You're not driven by selfish needs, Shanna. I know that. I don't think there's anything manipulative about you."

But there was, and that was when she realized it. She was here to use Ben as her means to being accepted back into the family, and into the medical center. Maybe she wasn't overtly using him, but using him as her role model to get something she wanted was its own brand of manipulation, and suddenly she felt ashamed. She should have been honest with him from the start, and take the consequences as they came. Now it was too late. Ben wasn't who she'd believed he was. Not at all. And to top that, she was falling in love with him.

"Look, I um..." Sliding to the floor, she paused for a moment, but couldn't find it in herself to look at him. "About tonight. I can't go to the village with you. And you do need your rest." She wanted to suggest another time, but she wasn't sure she should. Because to go much further with this, she'd have to tell him everything, and to do that would hurt a kind, decent man who didn't deserve to be hurt. *Hey, look, Ben. I came here to pattern myself after the coldhearted so-and-so I thought you were.* It made her sick to even think that had been her motivation.

"Anyway, I'm going to make sure Beatriz gets back home safely, then I've got some paperwork to catch up on. So…" There was nothing else to say, so she didn't. Sighing, she shook her head in despair, then walked out the door.

What was the point of any of it? It always turned out the same. He'd taken that step forward, and she'd stepped backward. He'd gone against his resolve, and it had turned out exactly the way he'd known it would. But there were times he just wanted to forget who he was, how he lived. Because, damn it, he was lonely. So lonely he had to force himself to face the next day. Every time he crawled out of his bed, it felt like something was ripping out his heart. And Shanna…he knew she wouldn't stay. But he'd wanted to forget that. Wanted to forget his past, forget everything.

But it didn't matter, did it? Or maybe it did. Because it hurt more than he'd expected as he hadn't been able to brace himself against her the way he did everything else. So, really, what *was* the point?

He was falling in love, which was tantamount to falling into a great abyss. That was the point.

CHAPTER NINE

"THEY'LL both be back next week," Ben explained to Shanna as the two of them shared a hasty breakfast at his tiny kitchen table, sipping coffee and eating *sandwiches di miga,* crustless sandwiches stuffed with red peppers, tomatoes, lettuce, ham and hard-boiled eggs. He was glad Amanda and Jack were returning to Caridad but concerned at the same time because, while his sister's pregnancy was textbook perfect, he knew she would throw herself into the work here the way she always did, and it worried him.

Of course, she was Jack's to worry about now. He was only the bystander, as it should be. In so many ways, though, he envied her the life she was building. Husband, son, baby on the way... he'd never dreamed of having those things. Why fool himself? Marriage, family, happily-ever-after bliss weren't in his future, and he'd known that for a very long time.

"So if I left, you wouldn't be in a bind?"

"You're thinking about leaving?" It didn't surprise him. Shanna needed more than this. She was too vital to contain here. He understood it, but he didn't like it.

"Maybe. Haven't really decided yet."

"Going back to Chicago? Back to your practice."

She shook her head. "I, um…I'm going back, but in a different direction. Going to step out of patient care, leave that for those more suited to it, and focus on hospital administration. Chief Operating Officer."

That surprised him. No, that shocked him. "Which means?"

"A lot of responsibility. I'll be accountable for the smooth and efficient operation of all our various facilities, including the management of the profit-and-loss statement for the hospital's business. I'll also oversee the integration of our strategic plan, and provide oversight for the development of high-quality, cost-effective and integrated clinical programs throughout Brooks Medical Center. Our management portfolio is diverse, Ben, and this position carries with it a substantial scope of obligation. It's a new position for Brooks Medical Center and my family feels it's best keeping it in the family."

"Then why are you here, working harder than you've probably ever worked in your life, telling me you want to be like me?"

"One last fling to see where I belong, I suppose."

"What you're telling me is that based on what you're doing here, you're going to return to Brooks and never see another patient again? How does that make sense, Shanna? Because that's not you. You love patient care. In fact, I don't think I've ever seen anyone love it the way you do. Anyone looking at you can see it. And anyone who knows you knows that not being in patient care will make you miserable. So why the change?"

"You adjusted to your life, Ben, based on your circumstances. That's all I'm doing—adjusting."

"But I didn't walk away from the one thing I truly love."

"I'm not walking away, either. Simply walking in another direction."

Something else was at the bottom of this because Shanna clearly did not want to make this move. Judging from the dismal look on her face, she knew it was a mistake. Yet for some reason he didn't know, she was about to go through with it. "Are you trying to get yourself even more lost?"

he asked. "Because the minute you put on your administrator hat, that's what's going to happen to you, and I think you know that.

"Some people are born to be great administrators, Shanna. But some are born to be great healers, and that's what you are. Your heart, your soul…it's all about the care of others, and if you walk away from it, you're going to regret it every day of your life. And the down-to-the-soul kind of misery you're going to feel can cause you to do things to yourself you'd never believed you could." Alcoholism. Drug addiction. And worse.

"No, I'm not trying to get myself any more lost because I'm not sure it's possible to be any more lost than I already am," she said on a dispirited sigh.

"Then why leave here? We may not have all the whistles and bells you have at Brooks, but I believe you know who you are here."

"Why leave?" she asked, then immediately countered with, "Why stay?"

"Because you love the work, you can't deny that."

"Yeah, well, I love lazy days on a tropical beach, too. But not enough to spend the rest of my life there. Besides, you'll be back to full coverage, so you're not going to need an extra doctor hanging around."

"Don't make this about what I need or don't need for Caridad. We always need doctors. That's probably never going to change. So why are you really doing this?" Why the hell couldn't he just bring himself to tell her he wanted her here? That he liked having her around? That she made him feel...she simply made him *feel?*

Because that would call for a step further, a commitment he didn't have in him. Oh, she'd stay out of pity, or some selfless act that bound her here only as a doctor, because that was who Shanna was. In the end, though, she'd quit looking at him the way she had when she'd kissed him, the way a lover did. Seeing that look die was something he couldn't bear. That was why he couldn't ask her or tell her or beg her to stay. Because she would, but for reasons that would only hurt her.

"You've got more than enough volunteers to cover, Ben, so you really don't need me."

"But it's nice having someone here for...for continuity's sake."

She laughed bitterly. "That's me. Standing right in there for continuity's sake." She glanced down at the sandwich she'd been nibbling at for the past twenty minutes, then tossed it across the room, hitting the trash can with it dead center. "Look, I'm not going to leave you in a lurch, if that's what you're worried about. I may wear my heart on my sleeve when it comes to dealing with my patients, but I'm responsible."

Ben pushed back from the table so abruptly his chair toppled as he stood. "Whoever said you weren't?"

"Outright? Nobody. By implication? My father and my grandfather. My mother, my grandmother. My brothers. See, I'm the one who didn't fit into the mold, and maybe that's some of that willfulness from my youth hanging on. Maybe it's not. I don't know. But I do know this. There comes a time when you have to meet your life head on. This is my time. And my life…it is what it is." She spun, headed for the door, got to the doorway then stopped, and turned to face him.

"I love Caridad, Ben. Love what you're doing here. For me, that's always the problem. I love, and it gets in the way. You, of all people, should understand that, because you've managed to push all the love in your life so far to the sides I doubt you could even see it from wherever you choose to stand."

While she hadn't meant that to be cruel, what she'd just said slapped him so hard he could almost feel the literal sting. It was true, of course. Just not easy to hear. Even more difficult knowing Shanna could see that in him.

"I, um…I spare other people's feelings," he said with much more composure than he felt. "Because I know how it is to come face-to-face with a flaw. That's what I am, Shanna. A flaw. And I accept that because while people may take pity on me for a little while, it doesn't last. So why put anybody through that? Why put myself through it when I know how it turns out in the end? So if you see that as shoving love aside, then that's what it is. But that's me. It's not you. Love doesn't get in your way. It's what makes you who you are…a doctor who exudes passion and compassion. Losing that to paperwork is…it's unfortunate. And wrong."

"But what happens, Ben, when the passion and compassion get in the way of good doctoring?"

Now he had the perfect picture, the perfect understanding of what her family had done to her, and it made him sick to his stomach. "You said you wear your heart on your sleeve."

She nodded. Swallowed hard. "That's me. Heart

on my sleeve. A real sissified practitioner because I get too emotionally involved."

"Who the hell ever said something like that to you?" Actually, he could guess. He'd met Miles Brooks once. Recognized his handiwork.

"It doesn't matter, because it's true. I get too involved. Lose objectivity."

"Your grandfather is wrong, Shanna. And it does matter. Your greatest ability is the way you empathize with your patients. You understand them in ways most doctors can't, and to berate that shows ignorance and intolerance. So why are you going back to a place where you can't be the kind of doctor you have a natural gift for being simply to try and fit yourself into a mold that will never fit you?"

"Because if I don't, it's not just my spot in the family medical practice I'll lose. It's my spot in the family. And in spite of who they are, or what they are, I don't want to walk away from them."

"Maybe you don't, but think about how they're willing to walk away from you. Look, Shanna, I know what it's like to have everything you've ever known taken away from you. After I was burned I spent a year, a complete year simply fighting to survive, and I gave up more times that I can probably remember. Not because of the pain, not because of the prospect of dozens of surgeries in my future, but because I knew that my old life was gone. I lost my youth, I lost my innocence and I lost everything I'd ever thought I would have in life because one simple thing I loved doing— working on cars with my dad—went bad in ways no one could have ever predicted.

"Trust me, it's not easy coming back from that loss. By the age of nineteen I was an alcoholic. Couldn't get through my day without bracing myself with a drink or two or ten. Then when that wasn't enough to get me through, I added drugs to that mix."

"Ben," she gasped, "I—I didn't know."

"Nobody does, outside my family. It was a bad time for all of us, but the point is I lost myself in profound ways I still don't understand. I couldn't figure out my day, let alone my life, because I was scared to death to face my loss. And that's what you're about to do. You're about to lose yourself in such a profound way because you're afraid to face the loss of your family. But the loss of Shanna Brooks is a far worse loss."

She swiped at the tears streaming down her cheeks as Ben crossed the room and pulled her into his arms. A place where she fit so naturally. It was a dangerous thing he was doing. But for the moment Shanna's need was greater than his, and nothing else mattered.

"You're a good man," Shanna finally said through her sniffles. She put her hand over his heart. "I don't know what you've suffered in the past, but you have too much goodness in your heart to shut out the people who see it, who want to be part of it." Her hand moved to the right, and came to rest on the buttons of his white camp shirt. "A few days ago, when I told you my goal was to lose myself..." She undid the top button of his shirt. "That's what you do, isn't it? Lose yourself, pray to God nobody finds you. It's no different than what I'm doing, is it? You isolate yourself in a jungle clinic for fear someone will get too close. I isolate myself in my family for fear they will turn their backs on me. Makes us quite a pair, doesn't it?"

There was nothing in him that was prepared to deal with this—with her brutal honesty. Because she was correct. It was easier being lost. "I tried the other way, and it didn't work."

She undid another button. "Because you didn't want it to work, Ben. You're a capable man.

Maybe the most capable person I've ever met, so you're not going to be stopped at anything you truly want to do."

He raised his hand to cover hers, to stop her unbuttoning his shirt, because what she'd find underneath was so obscene, and Shanna was so pure. "What I want is my practice here."

"And to be left alone," she said. "You forgot to add that part, Ben. You truly, sincerely want to be left alone. Want to be a recluse, live your life out without anybody coming close. Then someday Amanda's children can talk about their odd uncle, the one who spent his life in this one-room apartment and only came out to work." She drew in a shuddering breath, then let it out and looked up at him. "I show it all too easily, and you hide it all too easily."

Without provocation, without warning, she pulled her hand away from his, then grabbed hold of his shirt and literally ripped it open, exposing every bare inch of his chest.

"Damn it to hell," he grunted, grabbing at the fabric, trying to cover himself.

"No," she said, her voice almost a whisper as she grabbed his hand. "Don't, Ben."

"You don't understand..." Shoving her hands

off him, he spun around and literally broke into a run, to his bathroom, to his closet, anywhere to cover himself. Anywhere to get away.

But Shanna was too quick. She caught up, practically tackling him as she grabbed him from behind, and held on. Laid her head on his back, wrapped her arms around his waist and simply held on for dear life. For a minute, or an eternity…it all blended together. His needs, his desires, his reality… Then he snapped back to where he needed to be. "Don't do this, Shanna," he said. "Don't fool yourself into thinking that this could be something other than what it is. We're colleagues, that's all there is. That's all I do."

"But is it all you *want* to do?" she asked him. "Tell me the truth, Ben. Is that all you want of us?"

"All I want is…"

"To be left alone to practice your medicine. That's what you keep saying. And maybe you believe it. But I don't."

How could he do this? How could he walk away from her and not look back? He wanted her to stay. Wanted to live in the fantasy that everything would work out, that they could end up like Amanda and Jack, and work through the obstacles to find the love. But he knew better, because he knew himself. And Ben Robinson, as himself, was the one thing Shanna didn't know. She saw the doctor and the outward manifestations of the man, but the layers underneath were so grisly they would defy Shanna's usual sunshine optimism. To see that diminished or destroyed in her...he couldn't do it, because it was that optimism he'd first loved about her.

"We all make choices based on who we are, Shanna. It's one of those facts of life you can't escape."

Loosening her grip, she slid round to the front of him and gently pulled apart the ripped fabric of his shirt. "What if you make choices on the wrong perception of yourself?" Gently, so very gently, she traced her fingers over his chest, over his scars. "Could that be you, Ben? Could that be what you've done to yourself?"

Shutting his eyes, he was torn between the pure, physical want for her touch and the sure knowledge of what would come later. No one had ever come this close, no one had ever touched him this way. Not physically, not emotionally. From Shanna, he wanted it more than he'd ever wanted anything in his entire life. Being touched by her—

that was all there was. Just this moment. Only her touch. It had to stop, though. He had to stop it. Yet the struggle was so fierce... "What I've done to myself is what I had to do. And I don't fool myself about anything." So true. But it was a truth not meant for her.

"But you're more than your scars, Ben."

Her fingers fluttered up and down his chest, her touch so light he could barely feel it. But the shivers he was holding back and the pure emotional arousal told him she was there. Dangerously there. "And you're more than your family," he managed to say, fighting not to let himself sound as ragged as he felt. "Shanna, don't. We can't..."

Swallowing hard, he tried to step back, wanted to step back, but as he looked down and saw her eyes looking directly into his, there was nothing in him that could make him move. She was so beautiful, and so innocent. The ugliness of the world had never touched her and, with all his heart, he hoped it never would. "You don't know what's involved here. Don't know me..."

"Touch me, Ben," she said, taking hold of his hand and guiding it to her chest, over her heart. "That's what I know. I want you to touch me." He was such a beautiful man, in every way she wanted. She could see that beauty, and feel it every time she looked at him, yet how would she show him what was so obvious to her? "And I want to touch you."

Reaching up to his face, she followed the line of his scars, starting behind his left ear and twining down, under his chin, across his shoulder, his chest, over part of his stomach. Then, stopped by his cargo pants, she let that impede her only a moment, before she unzipped him, lowered his cargos and his briefs, and continued tracing her fingers across his lower abdomen, over his hip and came to a stop where his scar did, halfway down his thigh.

She felt him shudder, felt his muscles tense, knew if she looked up she'd see how rigidly his face was set, see how tightly closed his eyes were. None of that mattered, though, as she touched her lips to the start of the scar on his thigh and followed the journey upward her fingers had just traveled downward. But when she got to midchest, that was where she ended, where she snaked both her hands around his neck. Where he surrendered and his muscles relaxed. Where she lost her soul and found her heart.

* * *

It was still dark outside, but she was awake. Had barely slept, thinking about how this had started with her exploring the idea of leaving, and how beautifully it had ended, lying here with Ben. No matter how beautiful, though, she was filled with trepidation, this queasiness in the pit of her stomach that wouldn't go away.

Too many of her thoughts were wrapped in so much confusion because, come first light, everything would be the same as it had been before they'd spent the night together. They'd escaped into each other for a while, which had only deepened her feelings for this man. Nothing had changed, though. Not in any real sense.

And she wasn't going to delude herself into thinking that one perfect night would transform anything. Her family didn't want her the way she was, and Ben didn't want her. Those were two hard facts she still had to face.

Ben…beautiful man. Everything she'd ever wanted. Kind, considerate and so compassionate. Yet he was still so guarded. Not able to let himself go. Or only going through the correct motions. She'd felt it in the way he'd held her, kissed her, made love to her. He'd allowed her only a small part of him, but she wasn't even sure which part that was. She wondered if it was simply the physical need he'd relinquished to her when all she'd wanted had been a piece of his heart. Consequently, in the afterglow, the emptiness had started to creep in.

So for now she'd accept it as it was and, come daylight, maybe she'd see it all differently. Or maybe she'd pretend a little while longer that when Ben opened his eyes he'd see the possibilities, not the impossibilities.

Falling in love shouldn't be this difficult, she thought as she turned on her side to snuggle into Ben, who was likewise on his side but with his back to her. Scooting over, she matched the lines of her body to his and placed her hand over his waist, just to feel connected. Maybe that was what she'd missed—the real connection between them. Or maybe she was simply reading her insecurities into a place they didn't need to be. Whatever it was, duty would be calling in another couple of hours, and she needed to be better rested. So she exhaled, relaxed, enjoyed the feel of him pressed to her, and…

She felt his muscles go tense. Then jerk convulsively. One hard, fast snap. Then his breathing turned shallow for a moment, almost like he was panting, and she was instantly alert. Did he feel warm? Too warm? Another hard jerk followed immediately by a third one...

"Ben," she whispered, giving him a gentle nudge on the shoulder.

His response was a groggy mumble. Understandable. He was sleeping, didn't want to be disturbed. But she propped herself up on her elbow and instinctively reached over him to feel his forehead. An old-fashioned diagnostic tool, but it worked. And he wasn't just warm, he was burning up. "Ben," she said, this time giving him a hard shake.

Again, he responded with a mumble, so Shanna rolled over, flipped on the light on the bedside stand, then rolled back to Ben and pulled him over onto his back. "Ben," she said, this time urgently. "Can you hear me?"

His eyes fluttered open. "I'm fine," he said, his voice unusually gravelly.

"Look at me," she said as his eyes sagged closed again. "Focus on me, Ben. Open your eyes and focus on me." Moving up to her knees so she could get a better angle to examine him, it occurred to her that he was completely naked and except for Ben's T-shirt, which she was wearing, she was nearly the same. "Come on, open your eyes," she said, patting both sides of his face to arouse him.

"I already focused on you," he said, opening his eyes and attempting a smile.

"You have a fever. You've been telling me you were tired, that you weren't sick. But now you have a fever, and it's high, Ben. I don't know how high, but it's high."

"You make me hot." He shook himself, shook his head, sucked in a deep breath. "But I'm not sick. All I need is some sleep."

While his words weren't nearly as garbled now, he was still too thick, too lethargic. "How long have you been feeling bad?" she asked. Taking his pulse—too fast. Feeling the glands in his neck— slightly swollen.

Instead of answering, he went back to sleep.

"Ben, please. Stay with me."

"I can't," he mumbled. "What I did… Horrible things. Let people down…"

She needed to examine him. *Really* examine him. But she was torn between dressing and running across the hall for her medical bag or simply calling Dr. Hueber, the on-call for emergencies tonight, and letting him make the assumptions he wanted.

Except assumptions might not be good for Ben's reputation, and she didn't want to jeopardize his hospital or his standing in the village, so she threw on her clothes faster than she knew she could dress, dashed to her room across the hall, then hurried back and practically tumbled back into the bed next to him to take his blood pressure. Low. Respirations normal, but on the shallow side. Pupils reactive, but a little sluggish. No huge concerns so far. Then his heart, and that was where the concern started. His pulse was thready, cutting in and out.

An infection? She'd seen him tired, seen him avoid meals, claiming he was too busy to eat. Those might simply be Ben, but they might also be symptoms of whatever this was. "Ben," she said, giving him a gentle nudge. "Wake up. Hear me? Wake up. I want to ask you some questions."

"Need a shower," he mumbled. "Make morning rounds…"

"No morning rounds," she said, scrambling from the bed and rummaging through his drawer for a pair of briefs. Once found, she put them on him, along with socks. She had no reason why those were important to her, but they were. She wanted him to look…professional when she admitted him to the hospital. So after the socks, on went a scrub shirt and pants, and that was where she stopped and called Hueber, and told him what was going on. His response was to send two volunteers and a stretcher and, within minutes, Ben was stretched out atop an exam table, where Dr. Hueber was hooking him up to a heart monitor while Shanna was busy starting an IV.

"When did this start?" Hueber asked.

"He was fine last night. We talked for a while after our shifts were over. Then this morning, when I went to make sure he was on morning rounds, he was like this."

"Noticed anything before this? I've only been here a few days, so I haven't really had the chance to talk to him yet. But if you've been around awhile, maybe you've noticed something."

"Maybe. He's been tired off and on, and doesn't have much of an appetite."

"Been fine," Ben interjected. "Working too many hours."

"Working too many hours doesn't get you in this shape," Shanna said, glancing nervously at the heart monitor. "So tell me when you started feeling bad."

"A few minutes ago."

She glanced across at Hueber, who was getting ready to put an oxygen mask on Ben. "Now, be truthful with me, Ben. How long have you been feeling bad?"

This time he didn't answer. He simply sighed heavily and drifted off.

"I'm assuming he's current on all his vaccinations," Hueber said.

Shaking her head, Shanna shrugged. Honestly, she didn't know. Doctors were usually the worst patients so she wouldn't put it past Ben to let his vaccinations lapse. She hoped he hadn't, though, because that would be a starting point, where they could begin to rule out various conditions. She ran a hand over Ben's sweaty brow. "What have you done, Ben Robinson?" she asked, not concerned that Hueber was arching knowing eyebrows at her. "What did you go and contract?" And could they treat it here, or should they be looking for a lifeline out?

Hueber cleared his throat. "I don't suppose you've inspected him, have you?" he asked, then added, "In the professional sense."

"What do you mean?" she asked, the implication of Hueber's question not lost on her.

"For bites, cuts, rashes, those sorts of things. It's what we do here in the jungle because there are so many unknown variables we're not used to dealing with. You know, look between fingers and toes and all those other places you might not normally examine."

"No, I haven't inspected him. I only found him right before I called you." Technically, that was correct. Besides, it was none of Hueber's business that she'd spent the most amazing night of her life with Ben prior to that. At least, she hoped medical necessity wouldn't turn it into Hueber's business.

"Then while I go wake another doctor up to come work in Emergency, I'd suggest you inspect him. And keep your fingers crossed we find something easy to identify. Because Ben doesn't have the medical resources at Caridad yet to take care of him if we don't see something we can diagnose pretty damned fast, and have the means to treat." He sighed. "And don't fight me on this, but I'm going to line up medical transport for him in case we can't treat him here. Or he gets worse."

There wasn't an argument in her. What Ben was experiencing always came with the uncertainty of not knowing what came next. Truthfully, it excited her. Showed her a raw, new medical horizon she hadn't even known existed. In her heart of hearts she wanted to stay, wanted to be a part of everything Ben did here. Wanted to be a part of Ben. But staying came with the knowledge that she might never get from him what she needed, and how did someone who openly wore her heart on her sleeve survive that?

"What did this to you?" she asked as she examined his arms, first his left, then his right, noting the perfect flesh juxtaposed against the scars. "To have gone through what you did and get yourself to where you are…" Suddenly, the doctor in Shanna gave way to the woman, and she felt warm tears sliding down her cheeks. It didn't matter if Hueber saw, didn't matter what he knew. She was in love with this guy, didn't care if her heart *was* on her sleeve or if she was just plain sissified, like her grandfather had said.

Right now she needed to cry. For herself. For Ben. "When you're better, we've got some things to talk about, Ben Robinson," she managed through her sniffles.

He stirred. Opened his eyes and simply stared at her for a moment. Then he reached up and brushed a tear from her cheek. And went back to sleep before he could lower his hand to the bed.

She caught it as it dropped, and held on for a moment. "I'm going to get you through this," she promised, then kissed his hand and lowered it to his side. "Don't know what it is, but I'm a good doctor." Bending down to his ear, she whispered, "And you're a good lover. It's a combination we can work with, Ben. But you've got to get better first. Hear me? You've got to get better."

Rather than responding, Ben remained still, so for the next several minutes she searched him for anything that might indicate what was happening. But came up empty.

"His sister's here," Hueber said, poking his head through the curtain. "And her husband. They want to take over his case. Just thought you should know."

Shanna nodded, and as soon as Hueber was gone, she kissed Ben gently on the cheek. "I'll be back," she whispered. "I promise."

"What is it?" Amanda asked, the instant Shanna stepped into the hall.

"Don't know, so right now we're treating symptoms and watching him."

"That's not good enough!" Amanda snapped. Her husband, Jack, stepped up beside his wife and slipped a steadying arm around her waist.

"I'm Jack Kenner," he said, pulling his wife tight to his side.

"Nice to meet you. I'm Shanna Brooks."

"So, do you suspect anything?" Jack asked. "How was he acting before he got sick? Was he displaying any symptoms?"

"Tired, lack of appetite. Then this morning he spiked a fever, starting having a heart arrhythmia, compromised respiration. Became lethargic, not comatose but at times on the verge of going completely under. So far, though, he always rallies out of it. But each time it's dragging him deeper down."

"And you're sure these symptoms manifested themselves this morning?"

Shanna nodded, didn't say a word. But the implication wasn't lost on Amanda or Jack, both of whom had the good grace to not ask. "I've asked him a couple times lately if he's feeling okay, and he always said he's fine." She shrugged. "But that's Ben, isn't it?"

"I want Jack to treat him," Amanda said. "There's no time to soft-pedal this or spare feelings. Jack's the best, and I want Ben to have the best."

Shanna knew Amanda was upset, and didn't want to add to that, especially as she was pregnant. But she'd made a promise to Ben she intended to see through. Ben trusted that. Deep in her heart she knew he truly trusted that. "With all due respect, Amanda, I need Jack in the lab. He *is* the best, and he's the one who needs to do the tests. But I need to do the treatment because I promised Ben I would. So, if you'll excuse me, I'm going to draw the first round of blood work, so Jack can have a look."

"Can I see him?" Amanda asked.

"In a few minutes. I'm in the middle of an exam, and once I'm through with that, I'll let you know."

"He isn't going to…?"

Amanda didn't finish the question, but she didn't have to because the unspoken word congealed inside Shanna, clawed at her breath, clutched at her heart. "No. He isn't." Words that shouldn't have been said as last time she'd made that promise, she'd failed her patient. And if ever there was a time she'd worn her heart on her sleeve, this was it. It was time to face who she was, and accept it, for Ben. That was the thought weighing on her as she went back into the exam, followed by Jack, who insisted on drawing his own samples.

"In my work, it's best to control all the variables." He glanced briefly at Ben, then turned to the storage cabinet to pull out the various sample tubes he'd need and turned back. "Damned shame, what he's gone through," he said as he applied the tourniquet and started his search for a good vein. "He'd hate it, being exposed the way he is right now. Ben does everything he can to cover himself up."

"She's already seen me," Ben muttered.

Chuckling as he poked for a vein, Jack said, "So you're eavesdropping on us?"

"Some. Too much effort to open my eyes, but I can hear."

"Off and on," Shanna said, stepping up to the head of the bed with a damp cloth to wipe Ben's face.

"But everything was fine last night?" Jack asked. "And I'm not asking to pry. I need to establish a timeline."

"He was fine until a little before midnight, then…" Shanna shrugged, looked over at Jack, who was extracting his third tube of blood from Ben's arm, and smiled apologetically. "Then when

I woke up just after five he was like this. First thing I noticed was how hot he was, then after I checked him I discovered the rest." Dipping the rag into a basin of cool water, she wrung it out and began to wipe his face again, but stopped. Held her breath, bent down, took a close look… "Hello, kissing bug."

Also called a triatomine bug, they hid in crevices in the walls and roofs during the day, emerging at night when people slept. "See, Jack, right there, next to Ben's left eye, that little bit of swelling." The triatomine's choice of human contact— the face. Hence the common swelling near the eye.

"She knows bugs," Ben mumbled.

"I may know my bugs, but this little beauty isn't one of my favorites," she said. It caused too much damage. Often killed its victims or rendered them significantly damaged and disabled. Heart transplants were a frequent outcome for the lucky ones able to survive to that point.

The outlook for Ben? She hoped good. She hoped this was in an early enough phase that a sufficient course of benznidazole, an antiparasitic drug, would be all he needed. It was a long shot. She understood that. But she also knew Ben. He was strong. A fighter. If will could win this battle, he'd be good as new in due course. "Really, Ben. A bee sting would have been easier."

"Never claimed to be easy," he said as his eyes shut.

"No, you didn't," she whispered, then looked across at Jack, who was well into drawing the fourth and final tube of blood. "Jack, besides the blood work you're going to do, I'd like to get an abdominal X-ray, as well as do an endoscopy. Do you think Amanda will object?"

"You're Ben's physician," he said, "so do what you think is necessary. And, by the way, good catch, Dr. Brooks. I knew who you were before, but that officially turned you into a jungle doctor." After he'd drawn the blood, Jack pulled off the tourniquet then moved up to look at what Shanna had spotted. To the naked eye the swelling was nearly invisible. But it was there. He whistled as he palpated it with his index finger to make sure. "Yep. Hell of a good catch!"

"Well, it's barely there, but it's definitely a chagoma."

"And as it hasn't developed fully yet, I'm definitely impressed."

Maybe he was, but he needed to reserve judgment of her until later, after Ben had run his course with Chagas disease, so named for the Brazilian doctor who had first diagnosed it. Time, as well as treatment, would be the deciding factor, but time scared her to death as the course of this disease was to start mild in the early stages, sometimes go away altogether, sometimes go dormant, only to return with a vengeance after a while. Ben was definitely seeing the vengeance side, but she was praying it was the early stage of vengeance rather than the late.

"You stay with me, Ben," she told him three hours later, as she settled down into a chair next to his bed. "I don't want you going anywhere." They'd put him in one of the very few private rooms at Caridad after Jack had confirmed the diagnosis by identifying the parasites in Ben's blood, and after an abdominal X-ray and endoscopy had shown no intestinal, stomach or esophagus damage—the usual areas of damage in Chagas. And while Chagas wasn't contagious, and any other patient infected with it might have gone to the ward, Ben deserved his privacy. So much so, she believed, that she'd removed all the nurses from his care. He was hers to take care of, and hers alone.

So maybe it was the protective thing going on in her because Ben fought hard to protect himself. Or maybe it was just that she didn't want to leave him, didn't want to take her eyes off him. Didn't want to shut her eyes and not hear his breathing. Whatever the case, as she settled down she knew she'd be there for the duration, however long that was. After that…no clue. But for now her life was solved, even if that solution was only a temporary one. She loved this man and she was hoping the rest of it would fall into place.

"Damn it, Ben! I've spent a lifetime having difficult stuff, and for a change I needed something easy. But you're not easy. Not even close to it. So why did you happen to me?"

Naturally, he didn't answer. But that was okay, because she didn't have an answer, either. For now, maybe being clueless was enough.

CHAPTER TEN

"NOT as good as Italy," Ben said, struggling to his feet. Eleven days flat on his back, except for trips to the bathroom over the past couple of days, and he was ready to get up and move around. But slowly, because the repercussions from being bed-bound were screaming from every fiber and synapse in his body.

"What?" Shanna asked, holding on to him as she steadied him.

"Italy. The mountains, and the ski slopes. Nice way to spend my time off work. This wasn't. I hate being…"

She laughed. "Grounded."

"Grounded. Inactive. Treated like an invalid."

"But you are an invalid." They were heading outside, to a chair on the wooden porch.

"Because you've been waiting on me hand and foot. Being my *slave,* even though you didn't lose the bet." After he'd rejoined the so-called living, he hadn't really minded her taking care of him.

In fact, the better he felt, the more he'd enjoyed it. Shanna had such a feminine touch, and that was something he wasn't used to, especially when it touched him.

"Haven't heard you objecting."

"I've been sick, not crazy."

"Anything you want before I go on duty?"

Glancing over at the clinic, the line of people waiting to be seen was winding its way around the corner of the building. Ever since word had got out that he'd nearly succumbed to the dreaded kissing bug, people were lining up to have every bug bite and nibble checked. He couldn't blame them. It was a frightening thing to be attacked in the night and never even realize it until you were sick. Or, in his case, almost dead. "I want you to take some time off. You're looking worn out."

"Wish I could, but I can't. Your doctor is absolutely adamant about you not coming back to work for at least three more weeks, which means somebody's got to see your patients while you're sitting here lounging around and drinking tropical fruit drinks."

"My doctor is overreacting. I'll be good to go in a few days."

"Your doctor scheduled you for some tests in

Buenos Aires in a few days, and she's not taking no for an answer."

"I don't have any heart damage, Shanna," he said. Except for some residual weakness, he felt fine. Mentally, he was ready to get back to work, if not to active duty then consulting in some capacity. But she was being a real stickler, which he would appreciate for some other patient but not for himself. "All my vital organs are fine. Everything's fine."

"How do you know that, Ben? You were sick for weeks before you collapsed, and you didn't even know it."

"Because Chagas is asymptomatic in the beginning."

"Doesn't matter. I'm not clearing you for work, and that's hospital policy. Your policy. You have to secure your doctor's clearance to return to work after an extended illness."

He appreciated her diligence, but more than that he appreciated the feistiness in her. He'd been a grump these past several days and had caught himself arguing when there wasn't anything to argue about. Shanna had stood up to him every time, and he liked watching that in her. Part feistiness, part pure moral purpose. She was a fierce doctor. More than that, a true friend. Maybe the first one he'd had outside his sister since his childhood.

Loving her was complicating the situation, though, because things hadn't changed with him. At the end of all of Shanna's tender, loving care he'd still be who he'd been for the last dozen years, and she deserved more than that...better than that.

"I can change the rules."

A sly smile slid to her lips. "Not without Amanda's consent. And she won't consent, Ben. We're on the same page when it comes to what to do about you."

"I feel..." Happy, actually. *Happy* wasn't a word that invaded his vocabulary too often, neither did it ever have a place in his life. But he felt happy and in odd, refracted moments, even though he didn't want his convalescence to end. It had to, of course, but he liked the attention. Especially Shanna's attention.

"Smothered?" she asked.

"Picked on." In a good way.

"Poor Ben. Terrible patient. Even worse in his recovery." She laughed as she spun away. "If I have time, I'll join you for lunch. And if you need anything..."

"I need to get back to work."

"Not happening yet, so deal with it." She waved goodbye, then hurried over to the clinic where the waiting crowd almost mobbed her as she tried to get through.

Shanna had brought new life to Caridad. And new inspiration. The place needed her more than it needed most of the equipment on his want list because she embodied what he wanted this place to be—the hope, the passion, the caring demeanor. But she was fully in doctor mode right now, and when that wore down a little, when she actually had time to figure out that they weren't a couple, or involved, or could never have a relationship, she'd leave, because Shanna was such a bright star in the universe and Caridad couldn't contain her.

So for the next hour, trying to keep his mind off what he couldn't have, he sat in the sun and endured an article with the dry title "Internal Jugular Vein Cannulation: to Turn or Not to Turn the Head." Dry reading to go along with the title, and in spite of the early hour he caught himself nodding off halfway through, where he was just beginning to read the section where cannulation times, success rates and correlation to neutral head position and forty-five-degree head rotation were being introduced.

That was when his eyes finally gave up the battle and sent Ben off to catch forty winks, or in his case an hour's worth.

He only woke up when an unfamiliar voice invaded the pleasant dream where he and Shanna were stretched out on a blanket, having a picnic down at *laguna ocultada*. They'd just decided there were things better to do than eat when—

"Dr. Robinson?" It was an older voice, a vaguely familiar one. "You *are* Dr. Robinson, aren't you?"

He opened his eyes, disappointed that his dream had been interrupted. "I am," he said, looking up at the man. Good-looking guy, vaguely familiar face, lots of white hair, age indeterminable as he didn't have a wrinkle. But he had...Shanna's green eyes. He'd recognize them anywhere.

"And you're Dr. Brooks?" Extending his hand to the man, he didn't even attempt to stand. Wasn't sure if his legs were quite steady enough, and pitching forward into Shanna's grandfather's arms wasn't an impression he cared to make. "Please, forgive my appearance."

He had on his usual cargo pants and white, long-sleeved shirt, but his hair was unkempt, and he sported several days' worth of stubble. And he was barefooted. During his illness he'd discovered he liked going without shoes. A small step away from his cautious ways, but a nice one. "But I'm recovering from Chagas. Not up to speed yet."

"I trust it was caught early enough that you'll have full recovery," he said, taking Ben's hand. "Mind if I sit down?"

"By all means..." So, what was he doing here? Shanna hadn't mentioned anything about a visit. Or if she had, it had been days ago, when he'd still been too sick to hang on to much around him. Did she even know he was here? "Would you care for some fruit juice?" He pointed to the pitcher Shanna had left for him. "Or I can have some tea made. Yerba maté's quite tasty."

Miles Brooks rejected both offers and never fully settled into the chair. Instead, he sat on the edge, kept himself erect and, from outward appearances, aloof. His attire was something more suited to the golf course than the jungle. "My goal, young man, is to collect my granddaughter and leave here as quickly as possible."

"Shanna knows your plan?"

"What Shanna knows is that she doesn't belong here. She may have some wild, romantic notion that she's queen of the jungle, but her place is at her hospital, taking up her new duties, and once she's out of this environment, she'll remember that."

"You're really going to let her walk away from patient care to spend her days behind a desk?"

"Not let, young man. Insist. She has a good head for business matters, and a frail heart for patient care. What I've done is put her where she belongs."

"You put her where she belongs." No wonder Shanna was on a sabbatical. That was probably what he'd be doing too if Miles Brooks was what he had to face every day. "Shouldn't where she belongs be Shanna's choice?"

"When she works for me, no, it is not."

"Then that's too bad. Because I'd be willing to bet there's no one on your staff as suited for patient care as your granddaughter."

"I gave her the chance to be suited the way Brooks Medical Center needs her to be suited. But she failed, Dr. Robinson. Failed miserably."

"Failed what?" he asked.

"My ultimatum. After her sabbatical, she was to return to us as a doctor who didn't get emotionally involved with her patients, or as an administrator who would have no contact whatsoever with patients. Her emotions make her weak. She gets too involved, too caught up in aspects of a patient's life where she has no business. So I gave her a chance to correct that, to remove the emotion from her patient care and deal solely with the treatment. In other words, eliminate the involvement she seems to develop for the people she treats and simply do a straightforward job. It's what we expect from all our physicians, and Shanna is no exception.

"Oh, and she agreed to the arrangement, by the way. We didn't just shove her out the door. She walked away willingly, knowing what she had to do."

He didn't know how to process this yet. Didn't even know how to begin, he was so...numb. Shanna had agreed to her grandfather's ultimatum? How? Why? "And she's agreed to return to Brooks on your terms?" he asked, trying to blot out what was becoming glaringly obvious.

"If she doesn't return, the board has the right to sever her completely from Brooks, which would mean her part-ownership would dissolve."

"And she wouldn't be welcome in her family?"

"Really, that's none of your business, Doctor."

True, it wasn't. But now he had his answer and he couldn't simply blot it out. Because now he understood why Shanna had come here to be like him. In her eyes, he was like her grandfather. Cold, dispassionate. She'd come here to learn detachment from the master of detachment. He couldn't say it was a good feeling, being copied for the things he himself knew weren't good.

In fact, it felt downright awful, because he'd hoped she was here to observe and learn something else from him. Jungle medicine would have been okay. Running a small hospital would have been fine. Or maybe, in the wildest of all fantasies, she'd followed him here because she'd wanted to have some kind of a relationship, in spite of his platonic ways in Tuscany.

Well, it didn't matter what he thought, did it? Because what Shanna had come to learn from him was how to be a cold, impersonal bastard like her grandfather was. That was all she'd wanted—to figure out how to switch off her real self, the way he was so good at doing, and turn on the heart of stone. And she'd seen him as her perfect teacher. "You don't care what people want, do you, Dr. Brooks? Or what they're best suited for?"

"In my world, what I have to care about is that

everything is run as efficiently as possible. We're a large institution, and silly sentimentality gets in the way. Shanna suffers from silly sentimentality, and the only way to reduce that is to remove its cause from her path. I know you run a hospital here, but I doubt you can even begin to comprehend to enormity of the task of running Brooks."

No, he couldn't imagine. Neither did he want to. "How did you find Caridad?" he asked, fighting back the thought of what Shanna really thought about him.

"You're easy to track. And I do remember you, by the way. Young man with an axe to grind. My decision to refuse you for a residency was a good one and judging from the way you ended up, even better than I realized. You may think you're some kind of a Svengali, son, who's going to manipulate his way into the Brooks family and medical resources through my granddaughter, but it's not going to happen.

"It's a simple equation, really. Shanna back at Brooks Medical Center equals everything for her. Shanna staying at this little place you call Caridad equals nothing for her—no more partnering in our medical enterprises, no more position at the hospital, no more family, for the most part.

If she turns her back on us, we turn ours on her. And somehow I have an idea you enter into the equation, don't you? I'm sure she's gotten herself all emotional over you. Young man with a tragic past. Now with a serious illness. That's her element, Doctor. It's where she deludes herself into believing she's delivering good patient care."

"You're a divisive son of a bitch, Dr. Brooks."

Miles Brooks laughed aloud over that. "Been called worse, young man."

"But have you been called shortsighted? Because believing that good medicine is practiced without emotional involvement is about as shortsighted as it comes."

"Fine. Run your hospital on any kind of emotion you want. But don't disrespect me because I don't choose to be the same kind of administrator you are. What I do works."

"And hurts your granddaughter. Can't you see that? She's as gifted a doctor as I've ever seen, and what you expect from her either diminishes or disallows that. And if you force her back to Brooks in an administrative-only capacity, it's your loss."

"Or, depending on the perspective, my gain."

"Add manipulative to my description of you,

Dr. Brooks. Because it's not Shanna you want. It's your victory over her."

"It's never occurred to you that her family loves her and that's why we want her back."

"No, because it's never occurred to Shanna that her family loves her." He watched the old man's face for some sort of shock, or anger, because that was an outrageous statement to make, as true as it was. Sadly, nothing registered on Miles Brooks. And that was when it hit him again. Shanna had believed she could learn from him how to be like this cruel excuse of a man.

"What her family loves, Dr. Robinson, is any equation that betters the hospital. Shanna is part of that equation. But do you fall into that somewhere? To get her, do I have to offer you something?"

"Shanna's too smart to get involved with me because she sees me as being just like you. She deserves better than me, and better than you."

"See, that's where you're wrong. You're nothing like me, because men like me don't have women like my granddaughter falling in love with them."

She was in love with him? It was everything he wanted to know, and nothing he wanted to know.

Miles Brooks arched bushy eyebrows. "You

didn't know that? Because you conceal your feelings as poorly as my granddaughter does, which caused me to think you might pick up on the feelings of others as easily as she does. Doesn't matter, though. You'll stay here, she won't. She's a Brooks after all. We know where we belong. But I'm willing to make you part of this if that's how it turns out."

How it would turn out was that there was nothing for Shanna here, especially if what her grandfather said was true, that she loved him. And, damn, did that jar him. More than he expected. "Look, Shanna's in clinic right now, so please don't interrupt her while she's seeing patients. We're going to have lunch together in a while, and you're welcome to join us then. In the meantime, the brown building just to the front of the hospital has an empty room, and you're welcome to make yourself at home there, for as long as you stay at Caridad."

"Just for the night, son. That will give Shanna sufficient time to get her things packed, and for you to make your decision." With that, Miles Brooks stood, bowed slightly at the waist, and headed for the steps. "I understand that you're concerned for my granddaughter, and if you care for her the way I believe you do, you'll do what's best for her. So, please, have someone come and get me when Shanna is available."

Or never, Ben thought. *I'll never have someone come and get you, you manipulative old...*

"You're not supposed to be up and wandering around yet," Shanna said once she noticed Ben standing by the wall in her exam room, simply watching her bandage the lengthy cut to which she'd just applied twenty-two stitches on a little boy's left leg.

"I could have done those stitches. Simple thing, no physical effort."

"Or stayed put, like the doctor told you to do."

"I did, for a while. Read some. Had a visitor."

"Maybe you should have kept your visitor there longer so you'd have stayed down longer." She turned to face him. "Look, I know you're bored out of your head. I would be, too. But until we have some tests done that we can't do here, I want you resting. And we're not going to get them done until we can arrange a plane to get us there, which isn't until next week at the earliest. So, please, be a better patient."

He chuckled. "Deaf ears, Doctor. Your advice is falling on deaf ears."

"Don't I know that!" she said, then escorted the child out to the waiting room back to his mother. When she returned, Ben was seated on the exam table, legs dangling, the look on his face...well, she hadn't seen it before, couldn't determine what it was. But it was so serious it caused her to shiver. "You're not feeling well, are you?" she asked, stepping back into the room and shutting the door.

"I'm feeling fine," he said, patting the table next to him. "But we need to talk. I've already asked Dr. Hueber to cover the clinic for you for a little while so you don't have to worry about that."

"Maybe I should stand..." She didn't like bad news, and everything inside her screamed that this was bad. So bad, in fact, that last time she'd felt this way had been the day her grandfather had told her Elsa Willoughby had been turned down for a kidney transplant. That day had changed her life and, somehow, she knew this was going to be another life-changer. "Just tell me, Ben. Whatever it is, *please,* just tell me."

He patted the table again, and she climbed up next to him. Two people, sitting side by side, touching at the shoulders and hips, in an empty little room. Could have been intimate, but it wasn't. Ben knew that as he reached for Shanna's hand. Shanna knew that as she slipped her hand into his.

"Your grandfather is here," he finally said.

"What?" she sputtered.

"He was my visitor. He's come to take you home."

Of all the things Ben might have told her, this was the one thing she couldn't have anticipated. Her grandfather had come to get her. "Did he say why?"

"He said it's time."

"It's time because my family doesn't like to lose, and the longer I'm away from them the more they risk losing."

"Lose what? This isn't a game."

"Isn't it?" she snapped. Her body tensed. She could feel her muscles tighten, starting in her neck then working down to her shoulders, her back... "It's all about control, Ben. That's all it's ever about in my family, and I'm willing to bet my grandfather never once told you he'd missed me. And why my grandfather, Ben? I have parents— a mother and a father who could have asked me. Picked up a phone and asked. But they didn't be- cause that's not the way my family is run. And we *are* run, Ben. Make no mistake about that. We're run like a business."

"Which is why you left them?"

She shook her head. "When that's all you know, you accept it. It is what it is. And it really didn't bother me all that much, to be honest." When she'd been allowed to practice as a doctor and not as an administrator.

"Something bothered you enough to get you here, Shanna. And I know what it is now."

"To learn from you, Ben. That's what I've always said." Her heart started to pound because Ben had figured it out, and it hurt him the way she'd feared it would.

"And what I've never believed. But your grandfather told me about his ultimatum."

In spite of the Argentine heat in the room, she shivered. "I'm not sure..."

"Yes, you are. After your sabbatical you were to go back to Brooks either as a doctor who didn't get emotionally involved with her patients or as an administrator. One or the other. In fact, it was an agreement you made with your grandfather, wasn't it? Learn to be more like him or, as it turned out, like me? Me and your grandfather, one and the same."

"No, Ben. That's not what I was doing."

"Really, Shanna? Can you really sit here and tell me that you don't see me as a replica of your grandfather? That you didn't come here to copy me just so you could get back into his good graces?" He pulled his hand away from hers and stood. Went to the window and stared outside. "Because that's what it was. The one thing I couldn't figure out about why you wanted to learn from me. I flattered myself in a lot of ways, trying to figure it out. Or should I say, deluded myself?"

"You're not wrong," she conceded. "But you're also not right."

"Which makes about as much sense as everything else." He turned to face her. "Couldn't you have been honest and up front? Told me you'd come to learn from my cold, detached, harsh, heartless, indifferent, insensitive, uncaring, unemotional, unloving, unsympathetic ways—take your pick, use one description or use them all because they all work. They're all what you think of me."

"What I thought of you, Ben."

"Like I said."

This couldn't be happening. She'd almost convinced herself she could stay here, do the work she loved, coexist with the man she loved even though he'd never return those same feelings. Because having even a small piece of Ben was better than not having him at all. Which was, ironically, where she was now.

She couldn't blame him for being hurt, though, because yes, those were the things she'd thought he was, the reason she'd come here. But the reason she'd fallen in love with him had been because he was none of those things.

"What else was I supposed to think of you?" she asked, fighting not to cry, not to drag the emotions into this that had gotten her into trouble in the first place. "In Italy, we shared time together yet you kept your distance. You did the polite, expected things, like opened doors for me, and deferred to my lunch choices. But you kept this icy distance. And, yes, I thought you would be the perfect role model for what I needed to accomplish if I wanted to go back to my hospital...*my* hospital, Ben. It's all I know. All I ever wanted to do was grow up and be like the rest of my family. And you seemed...like the rest of my family.

"So I thought maybe observing someone like them outside the whole Brooks atmosphere might be what I needed. You know, keep it objective. Do it someplace where there weren't so many expectations of me. So I chose you. After I met you, I thought you'd be the perfect person to observe. Someone exceptional in his skills yet separated by an emotional mile from everything but the pure aspects of doctoring."

"See, that's what I don't understand. Why do you want to separate yourself that way?"

She smiled sadly. "It gets in the way."

"How, Shanna? Tell me how?"

"I've always loved the connections we have as doctors, Ben. You know that about me. It's why I'm happy in family practice because I can have those connections. In medicine, we're fortunate because we can touch so many lives, connect to so many people. I truly believe, in ways I don't understand, that everybody is connected. Maybe it's as vague as we're simply connected by the universe, or maybe there's this personal connection we have to find for ourselves. Whatever it is, I like that connection, and tried really hard to find it with everyone I took care of.

"But then there was this patient...Elsa Willoughby. End-stage renal. I told you about her. Anyway, I was furious my grandfather took her off the kidney transplant waiting list. *Furious.*

Because she might have had a good outcome. I wanted so badly for her to live that my objectivity was totally clouded by my emotional attachment."

"Age aside, was she a bad risk?"

Shanna nodded. "Medically, she had problems. But I cared for her, and because of that I made promises I couldn't keep. Then she died, and I…"

Okay, so the emotional block didn't work. Now there were tears running down her cheeks, and she didn't give a damn. "See, this is who I am," she said, swatting at the tears. "I lead with my heart and I can't change it. Although for a minute I thought if I watched you, I might find out how you did it, but you don't, Ben."

She sniffled. Looked up at him through blurry eyes. "You don't turn it off. None of it. You channel it differently, but you're not like my grandfather or any of the other people I've tried to emulate. I saw that in you almost immediately, and should probably have walked away before it came to…to this. Because, yes, I always knew I was going back to Brooks. That was the agreement. Return one way or the other."

"So you're going to return to something that will make you miserable?"

"We all learn to adapt, don't we? Just look at you."

"Did it ever occur to you, Shanna, that your emotional attachment to your patients is what makes you the extraordinary doctor you are? I've watched you, envied your confidence to become involved on the level you do."

"You don't have to be kind to me, Ben. I'll be fine."

"But will you be happy?"

Truly happy? No. Not without Ben. But Ben wasn't available, and the part of him she might have had earlier had vanished. "*Happy* is such a relative term."

"Okay, then skip happy. Will you be fulfilled?"

"Why do you care?"

"Because I care about you, Shanna. I'll admit I'm not sure how to get past all those things you thought I was, but that doesn't change the fact that I care about you, and I see you diving headfirst into the worst mistake you're ever going to make."

"So, what's my alternative? Stay here and work with the man I've fallen in love with, always knowing he doesn't want me? How does that make me happy or fulfill me?"

"You what?"

"Love you, Ben. And don't pretend you didn't know it. You did. But because you're not open to it, you've ignored it. But I don't hide things well, and you're not oblivious."

He sighed deeply. "Whatever you think you feel…"

"*Think* I feel? Whatever I *think* I feel? How can you say that to me?"

He sighed deeply again, and this time outwardly braced himself. "I've told you ever since you got here…"

She thrust out her hand to stop him. "It doesn't matter what you told me. Okay? Once again, I led with my emotions, and look where it got me. So why not go back to Brooks and be what I'm supposed to be?"

"Because it's not what you want to be."

"But I don't get to choose what I want to be, Ben. Wearing my heart on my sleeve the way I've been accused of doing so often hurts. And I can't be good at anything if that always gets in my way."

"Don't let it get in your way, Shanna. Embrace it."

"To what end? Because all I want is to embrace

you, and a life here at Caridad with you. But you won't let me have that."

"Which is what I've been saying all along. I can't get involved with you the way you want to get involved with me."

"Because of your scars? Or the fact that you had a problem with alcohol in the past? Do you think so little of me, Ben, that I can't get past those things?"

"No, I think so much of you, because I know you can. I'm the one who can't. Every time I look in the mirror…it's there, staring back at me. And if you thought all those horrible things of me be-fore… Shanna, there are parts of me that are dead. Nobody wants that around them. I don't want it around me, but that's how it is. How I am."

"Not dead, Ben. Maybe held back, but you have such a pure passion for medicine on a level I didn't even know was out there. I mean, here you are, this doctor who built a hospital out of a board and a couple of nails. There's nothing dead in that. And nothing dead in the man who made it hap-pen, and succeed."

Good argument on deaf ears. She could see that in him, see him pull back emotionally. In his mind he was distancing himself even more, and that was what she couldn't endure. He wouldn't let her in. More than that, he fought to keep her out.

"You know, I was willing to take anything just to stay with you. I love the medicine here, and I love you, and I would have taken whatever you allowed me. But you're not allowing me anything, Ben. Nothing." So maybe it was time to go, to end it. To do some of that distancing herself, so she could figure out what came next. Because it wasn't Brooks.

Ben had shown her who she was, as surely as he'd shown her he didn't want her. Loving Ben had made her realize who she wanted to be, though. But it had also shown her what she'd never have, and she couldn't stay here, facing that pain every day. "Anyway, unless you need me, I'll be packed and out of here by tomorrow."

"You're welcome to stay and work. Caridad needs you, Shanna."

"But you don't. I'm sorry if I hurt you, Ben. All those things I thought about you as a doctor were wrong. You're amazing, and I hope you have a happy life. Oh, and just so you'll know, I'm not going back to Brooks, because you're right. The kind of doctor I am is fine. That's what you've taught me, and for that I thank you."

* * *

She loved Tuscany in the winter, and she was glad it was still winter here. Loved the amazing slopes of Garfagnana, even though she hadn't done any skiing since she'd arrived two weeks ago. Loved the Tuscan wines, even though she hadn't drunk any on this stay. Loved the fairy-tale villages, age-old churches, hermitages, castles and fortresses, although she didn't feel up to exploring them just now. But she loved Tuscany, just not as much as Argentina. Argentina was her past, however. Its memories her heartbreak.

This morning she simply didn't have the will to move away from this table. *Their table by the window.* Some might call her crazy, sitting there, thinking of it as their table, but it was. She could still feel Ben here, and that was where she needed to be for a while—in a place where she could still feel him. Love lingering, love dying, neither was easy.

But she didn't know how to move on yet. Maybe because she didn't want to, or because the anchor of losing the life she loved wouldn't allow it. Either way, she'd come here every morning the way she used to, and stare at the mountain. Sometimes she stared for minutes, sometimes hours. Then the rest of her day was lost in aimless strolling, uneaten meals and forced smiles for those who greeted her.

She wanted her purpose back, and Ben and Caridad were her purpose. Except she was unwanted there, even though there had been a time she'd believed that Ben loved her and, in the end, that love would break away everything that held him back. But that had been an illusion the way everything else had been. Two weeks ago, when she'd walked away, part of her had clung to the hope he'd run after her. He hadn't. Hadn't reached out to her in any way. And that wasn't an illusion. It was a reality, the one he'd tried to convey to her, and she wouldn't see. Yep, heart on her sleeve all the way. Too bad she couldn't have traded it in for blinkers, but what was done was done.

So now this emotional aftermath was hers to deal with, and the most she wanted to deal with was this table, this window, and the mountain she could see from it. Sighing, Shanna shut her eyes, trying to block out all the images that didn't want to be blocked.

"Is this seat taken?"

His voice came to her so clearly she could feel the tears welling behind her closed eyes. "No," she whispered, wishing the memory wasn't so vivid. By now it should have faded. She wanted it to fade.

"It's the only table with a view of the mountain, and I love to sit and watch it. It makes me feel like a part of something important."

It was so real, the memory of that day, the words she'd said to him, his voice... She opened her eyes, hoped he was there. But he wasn't. So she closed her eyes again, this time not even trying to hold back the tears that were starting to fall. *Please, go away,* she thought. *How can I get over you if I can't get away from you?*

"I'd never really looked at those mountains from this window, though. Not before you pointed them out to me."

"Ben," she choked, spinning around to find him standing behind her. "You... What...? Why are you here?"

"It seems I have a doctor who wants me to rest. So I came here to rest."

"Your doctor wouldn't have approved your trip halfway around the world. Not yet."

"He's a competent doctor. Great cardiologist. Pronounced me in good shape, no permanent damage. But in bad need of some serious relaxation. Thought Tuscany was a great idea."

"You went for your tests?" she asked.

"Actually, I caught a ride with your grandfather. You left before he did, and he had room to take me. Having a jet at your disposal comes with some advantages. He dropped me off in Buenos Aires on his way back to Chicago." Smiling, he said, "May I join you, Shanna?"

Oh, how she wanted him to. But he scared her, and she already hurt so badly. "I was just getting ready to leave, so you can have the table to yourself. It's better than sitting in the back, staring at the wall."

"What if I want to sit here at this table and stare at you?"

"But you don't, Ben." She swiped away the tears on her cheeks. Drew in a bracing breath. Squared her shoulders to face the hardest thing she'd ever had to do—reject Ben. Not for herself, though. For Ben. "Maybe you think you're doing the right thing, or trying to end something that never got started, but you don't have to do that. I lost my way for a little while, but I'm fine now."

"Which is why you're sitting here, crying?" He stepped around her, and took that seat. Then reached across the table and wiped away a stray tear with his thumb. "I'm sorry, Shanna. I knew you were falling in love with me, and I supposed there was a huge part of me that wanted you to."

Finally, she looked into his eyes. "But the warning was out there, Ben. It was always out there. Even that night when we made love, you didn't let me have all of you. I knew it. Didn't want to see it. But I did know it."

"But you didn't know me, Shanna."

"And I've apologized for that. I was wrong for assuming…anything."

He shook his head. "You were right for assuming everything. It's what I put out there for people to see, and you saw it. But only part of it."

"The part you wouldn't let me see."

"The part I couldn't let you see."

"Why not?"

"Because to admit it to you is to admit it to myself. And after I admit it, then I have to come to terms with how it's a part of me that doesn't fit into anything good, or noble, or all the things you think I am. It's a hard thing to do, see a flaw that can never be fixed. It's easier to ignore it than admit to it, because…"

"Because admitting it shatters the barriers

you've put up around yourself to protect yourself from it. Then all that's left is vulnerability, and vulnerability can turn into such a deep, abiding pain if it's not tended properly."

"You're always amazing, Dr. Brooks."

"Not amazing, Dr. Robinson. Connected. And there's nothing wrong with that, as someone once told me. The thing is, all I've ever wanted in my life is to fit somewhere…somewhere I love, somewhere I want to be. And that was with you, which made me so vulnerable, because you shut me out every time I got close.

"Sure, maybe I could have hung around Caridad longer, waged a harder battle to get what I wanted from you, but what I've figured out is that I shouldn't have to fight for it. I fell in love with you for more reasons than I can count, and I'm still in love with you. I think you're in love with me, or you wouldn't have followed me halfway around the world. The feelings I have for you scare me, though, because you're who makes me vulnerable. But loving you makes me happy and hopeful. It's the same with you, I think.

"Loving me makes you vulnerable. But for you the remedy for that is to shut people out when they get too close. You shut me out because you don't know what to do with that vulnerability, and I don't want any more of that."

"It's conditioned in me, Shanna. Not meant to hurt anybody, but…"

"But protect yourself. I understand. People can be cruel, and I'm sure you've experienced more than your share of cruelty. So you keep yourself separate, push people away—"

"To protect them," he interrupted. "Them. Not me."

"Because you have scars? I don't understand."

"Scars," he said. "Deep scars."

"But this isn't about your physical scars, is it? It can't be, because that would make you…shallow. And you're not. So, who do you think I fell in love with, Ben?"

"You fell in love with an image. Someone you think is me, or you want to be me. But someone who isn't me."

"Who isn't you? The man in the café that morning who was so befuddled when a stranger sat down with him that he didn't know what to do? Or the man who spent the night knocking on doors, giving yellow-fever vaccinations to people who'd already refused them? Or spent the night, sitting in the chair at Maritza's bedside, watching her breathe, checking her pulse, reading—in very bad Spanish—bedtime stories to her?

"Tell me, Ben, which one of those people isn't you? Because the man who did all that is the one I fell in love with, the one I watched, and admired and realized he was worth everything I might lose if I stayed with him. And I want to stay with him, Ben. Now, even when I know you don't want me, I still want to stay with you, be a part of everything you are. Yet you're still pushing me away. You came all the way to Italy after me, and you're still shutting me out."

"You don't want to be part of everything, Shanna, because you don't know everything. And that's what I had to settle with myself before I came after you. What I had to face down in the mirror. Because you deserve to know everything."

"You mean before you push me away again?" she asked, withdrawing her hand from his. Glancing out at the mountain, she saw such majesty there. Looming over the entire village, it looked after the people, protected them, sheltered them, the way Ben did the people who came to Caridad. Yet there was a deadliness to the mountain. The snow that could take an inexperienced skier. The avalanche that could swallow up an unsuspecting village. No blame went to the mountain for these things, as the mountain lived up to its legacy.

So did Ben, and because she trusted in him with all her heart, she truly believed that no blame could go to him for whatever he perceived as his own deadliness. "You're right. I deserve to know," she finally said, hoping he understood where this had to go. Because this was up to Ben now. The rest of it was his to deal with because she'd gone as far as she could go. Loving him the way she did meant she would support him in anything, but he had to step up to take that support. With everything in her, she hoped he would.

"You flew from Argentina to Italy, but there's still one more step to take." The step where he proved his trust. Because in that trust she would find where she truly wanted to be.

He smiled, but sadly. "You see through me, don't you?"

"Not through you. But what I see encompasses some of you. It has to encompass all of you, though. And you have to be the one to allow it."

"Or it encompasses none of me, which you'll understand when you know *everything*."

"That sells me short, Ben. After I've told you my feelings for you, I don't deserve that." Rather than responding, he stared out the window for a few moments. Were his eyes focused on the mountain, or on something so distant she couldn't begin to fathom it? She didn't know, so she waited because, ultimately, this would have to be in Ben's good time, or not at all. So, two, three, four minutes ticked off the clock in utter silence as she watched him barely blink, barely breathe.

Then it happened. He drew in a deep breath, held it for a second, and let it out. "You're right. You don't deserve to be sold short, and I'm sorry you thought that's what I was doing." Finally he faced her again. "I wasn't. But you were right when you said you scare me, because you do. More than anything in my life ever has."

"Why, Ben?"

"Because you make me realize I have to face things in myself that I've never faced. Ugly things, things I've done, things I don't want to be part of me but are."

"You're not alone, you know."

He nodded. "I know. And maybe that's what scares me most. I know how to be alone. Do a pretty damn good job of it. Anything else..." He shrugged. Shook his head. Drew in another deep breath and let it out. "I was burned, as you already know. Had thirty-three surgeries, and survived in spite of some pretty overwhelming odds against me. That's really just the preface, because the real story starts later, after those surgeries.

"It was this never-ending grind, going from one surgery to another, never having a life in between. But I managed it. Managed to move on, go to college, get myself into medical school. Deluded myself into thinking that my life could be normal, in spite of the stares and the things people said behind my back. Or even to my face. But people will talk, won't they? Most of the time I just shut it out. It was hard to do at first, but after a while it became easy.

"Then I met Nancy. Nice girl. Not the love of my life by a long shot, but I honestly believed I could find something with her. Long story short, my shirt came off, she gasped, drew back in unadulterated repulsion, and that's when I knew that I couldn't shut it out, that people would always react the way Nancy did. Which was an excuse. It wasn't Nancy's reaction that mattered. It was mine. I just found it easier to blame the whole succession of events that followed on the easiest target."

"Events, like drinking?"

He nodded. "It's easy to shut out a lot of the world when you're drunk. But I never could get drunk enough, so I started taking pills. I'm a doctor, had doctor friends. Easy access to whatever I wanted to medicate myself with. End result, an alcoholic who was also addicted to drugs.

"Two years of it, Shanna. Two years of wallowing. I managed to live my life through the first year of it, but couldn't keep going during the second year of it and got myself kicked out of my residency. It wasn't that I didn't want to be a surgeon. I was in the program, and got kicked out of it because being a surgeon didn't really work well with who I was turning into."

"But you pulled yourself out of it."

"Not at first. I took a year, and simply wallowed. The more I wallowed, the more miserable I was. Vicious circle. I tried a couple of twelve-step programs and failed. Reapplied to a surgical residency, was turned down. Decided to skip surgery and try for family practice, and your grandfather turned me down."

"You went to another hospital, though. You said it was a better fit for you."

"I went there as an outpatient in their drug and alcohol rehab clinic, ended up doing some vol-

unteer work, then accepted a residency because
no one else wanted to work there. It was old and
underfunded and difficult, and they took me because no one else wanted the position. I will say
it was the best thing for me because I saw medicine from a perspective I'd never have found at
Brooks, and that's what made me able to come
here and do what I do. But the way I was accepted
there wasn't as a bright and shining endorsement
of anything."

"Except a commitment to move forward despite
the circumstances."

"See, that's the thing. I didn't have that kind of
commitment. Before I ended up there, I'd got to
the end of my rope, didn't see a way out. I was
drinking, I needed pills just to get me moving,
and my medical career was washed up. Nothing
in that mess was moving forward."

"But look where you are. How did that person
turn into the one who got you to Caridad?"

"Suicide. Or, shall I say, suicide attempt."

She gasped.

"What your grandfather turned down that day,
Shanna, was me, at the bitter end. I went back
to my hotel room, blamed him, blamed Nancy
blamed the world for the way I felt. Drank some

more, popped more pills. I was just so…tired. So defeated. The worse I felt, the more I needed the crutches that were destroying my life—booze and pills. I can't even begin to realize, after all this time, the lengths I went to when I needed to find that numbness. A stronger man might have faced his fate earlier on, but I wasn't a stronger man. I was the man who made excuses.

"That's all I did until the day I quit. And don't get your hopes up about me. It wasn't a moment of clarity, or some great manifestation of what my life could become if I let my tragedy work for me. You know, make me stronger. In fact, what happened was one of the least noble incidents of my life. I…I…"

Shanna swallowed hard, suddenly understanding where this was leading to. The inevitable ending to the kinds of suffering he'd gone through. "You tried to kill yourself."

"I thought about it. Spent days and nights planning it. Even went out to this hilly area where I used to play when I was a kid and climbed up to the top of one of the peaks, and thought about stepping off. Must have stood on the edge a good two hours, looking down at what could have easily been my destiny. One step, and everything would have been solved."

"What stopped you?"

He chuckled, but bitterly. "Ironically, after all my self-destructive behavior, it turned out I didn't want to die. I'd worked too hard for too long trying to live, and here I was, on the verge of taking one step farther because… You pick an excuse. I had a lot of them, and they all centered on somebody else doing something to me when I was the one doing it to myself.

"That's when it all became clear. No voices booming at me from the heavens, no lightning bolts. Just some pretty deep soul-searching and the discovery that the world was full of people suffering far worse than me, who didn't give up, and who succeeded in doing what they wanted in spite of their suffering Then there I was, always looking for the easiest way out. The epitome of weakness."

"Or maybe that was the time when your true character decided to develop. We all get there in different ways, Ben. For some people it's easy. Who they are just manifests itself. But for others the journey is so hard. Maybe because what you're supposed to do in life is so immense, or difficult you need to learn to deal with the adversities before you can accomplish great things."

"Yeah, well, tell that to my mirror, because every time I look in it, the person looking back looks weak to me. That's the monster I see, Shanna. Not the scars. Me. I know who I was, who I could become again. For me, every single day of my life is spent close to the edge. I'm still looking down, wondering what it would take to make me take that one step farther. How can I ask someone to be part of that?"

"But I know who you are, Ben. And when you're looking in the mirror seeing weakness, I'm looking in that same mirror at you, and all I see is unbelievable strength. To go from where you were to where you are now... Going through rehab, fighting to get back into a residency program. Setting up a hospital in Argentina. That's what someone in your life would be part of. What I would be part of, if you let me."

"That's what I want, Shanna. But what if I backslide? That's always a possibility. The biggest fear in my life. They teach you in the twelve-step programs that you're really only a step away from it at any given day, any given time. And it was so ugly. I was so ugly."

"Do you want to be with me, Ben?"

"More than anything. I want a future with you."

"Do you see marriage in that future?"

"I think I wanted to marry you the first time we sat here at this table together and you scared me so badly I ran to the back of the room to stare at the wall. But it's not that simple."

"I walked away from my life. Gave up a lot, actually. Stepped outside a medical practice I knew into something I had no idea existed. Turned my back on my family, who will now probably turn their backs on me. Fell in love with the most impossibly stubborn man I could have found, who loves me back but won't do anything about it. And you think that's simple?"

She scooted herself back from the table, then stood. "You know what? I'm tired of looking up at that mountain, wondering what's up there. Life's short, and we're wasting time. It's time to find out." She held out her hand to him. "I'm with you, Ben. But are you with me?"

Ben stood, then took her hand. "I'm with you."

"For the whole journey? Because that's what it's about. The whole journey or nothing."

He nodded. "I *am* tired of looking up at the mountain. I'm ready for the whole journey."

They stepped outside the café, and simply stood on the curb, looking up at the mountain together, Ben's arms wrapped around Shanna and Shanna leaning back into his embrace. "It's a long way up there," he finally said. "It'll take an hour to get to the lift and, depending on the lines of people, it might take us another hour to get to the top."

"Maybe even two or three," she added.

"Four. I think it's at least four."

"Then what do you suggest, Ben Robinson?" she asked, spinning round to face him.

"We get an earlier start at it tomorrow. But for now I know this bed and breakfast just up the street. Happen to have a room there, which I could probably switch to the honeymoon suite."

"That's what you want?" she asked him. "Are you sure? Because I haven't even heard a marriage proposal yet. So don't you think a honeymoon suite is getting ahead of ourselves?" She looked at his face, and for the first time since she'd known him saw no hesitance there. No distance. Nothing there but the glow of love, and trust, and the sure knowledge that this was where he belonged, where she belonged, where they belonged. And where they finally started, together. "So, will you marry me, Ben?"

"I thought you'd never ask." He pulled two boxes from his pocket and opened them. Wedding rings. Plain gold bands. "The custom is to wear the wedding band on your right hand until the wedding, when the priest blesses them and we move them to the left hand. These belonged to my grandparents, so they may look a little worn…"

"They're beautiful," she gasped as he took his grandmother's ring from the velvet box and placed it on Shanna's right ring finger, then kissed it. She did the same for him, and there, standing on a public street outside a little café, they made vows to each other. No priest, no formality, no legality. "I promise to love you and stand by your side forever, Ben Robinson."

"And I promise to love you and never shut you out of my life, forever, Shanna Brooks."

The traditional wedding kiss was a little salty for a quiet Italian village, but when they realized that they really did need to head straight to the bed and breakfast, in a hurry, and stepped back from each other, the small crowd that had gathered applauded them. Ben took a bow, Shanna curtsied, then they turned and strolled hand in hand to Signora Palmadessa's, where she threw rose petals on them when they entered.

"Almost a honeymoon," Ben whispered, as they sailed past the woman.

Shanna shook her head. Held up her ring, and smiled. "Doesn't matter which hand it's on. This is a real honeymoon."

"It's been sitting out there since this morning," she said, her focus on the large, wooden packing crate that had miraculously made it to Caridad. "Addressed to me. So I want to open it."

Ben laughed. Married legitimately a month now, he was only just beginning to understand Shanna and all her habits and personality quirks. It was a lifetime journey, he supposed, and one he was happy to take because marriage to her was everything he'd expected it to be. And so much more. In moments like these it made him wonder why he hadn't just married her at first sight then figured out the rough patches along the way, because doing everything together was so much better than being alone. "So open it," he said, handing her a pry bar then stepping back to watch.

"You don't think I can do it, do you?"

"What I think is that you can do anything you want."

She'd defied her family yet they'd come to

Argentina for the wedding. A simple affair, really, where they'd moved the rings to their left
hands, where she'd worn the traditional Argentinian blue petticoat under her white dress, where
they'd danced the tango half the night. Her family
hadn't stayed for the festivities. They'd literally
flown in for the ceremony then left immediately
after, but it was a start for Shanna, and she was
cautiously optimistic for the future. Her grandfather had mentioned wanting a first great-grand-
child. And he'd paid to have Ben's cottage with
two separate apartments renovated into a single
cottage for the two of them.

So maybe there were new things to explore with
her family now that she wasn't part of the family
business. However it happened, there were possibilities she'd never expected, and she was excited
to explore them.

"I can't even budge the crate, Ben. It must have
cost a fortune to have it shipped."

"It did," he said, grinning.

After taking several good whacks at the crate's
top and loosening some of its nails, Shanna finally
managed to wrestle the top of the box off, only
to find it packed with foam peanuts and packing
bubbles. But she tore at those like a woman pos-

sessed, throwing them all over the porch in her attempt to discover what was under them. Eventually, she saw it. "Ben, I..."

"You're not speechless, are you?" he teased. "Because if you are, I think I'll run and get the camera, because I'm not likely to see it again."

"How did you do this?"

"Bought it when we were in Tuscany, paid a company to ship it home—snail's-pace mail because I couldn't afford to express ship it."

She swiped at a tear sliding down her cheek. "It's ours, isn't it? Where we..."

"Met. Our table. Where we met. Where I fell in love with you." He'd bought the café table and chairs. "I didn't like the idea of other people sitting there, maybe damaging it or destroying it. Then I wondered about what would happen to it if the café changed its decor. So I bought it."

"Our table," she said, then ran across the porch, straight into Ben's arms. "Thank you, Ben. You don't know what this means to me."

"Want to show me?"

"In the middle of the day? You've got patients to see."

"Covered."

"And I'm behind on my charting."

"Charting can wait." He lowered his lips to hers. "Forever, for all I care."

"Why, Ben Robinson, whatever has come over you?"

"You," he said as his lips found hers.

* * * * *

Mills & Boon® Large Print Medical

September

NYC ANGELS: REDEEMING THE PLAYBOY	Carol Marinelli
NYC ANGELS: HEIRESS'S BABY SCANDAL	Janice Lynn
ST PIRAN'S: THE WEDDING!	Alison Roberts
SYDNEY HARBOUR HOSPITAL: EVIE'S BOMBSHELL	Amy Andrews
THE PRINCE WHO CHARMED HER	Fiona McArthur
HIS HIDDEN AMERICAN BEAUTY	Connie Cox

October

NYC ANGELS: UNMASKING DR SERIOUS	Laura Iding
NYC ANGELS: THE WALLFLOWER'S SECRET	Susan Carlisle
CINDERELLA OF HARLEY STREET	Anne Fraser
YOU, ME AND A FAMILY	Sue MacKay
THEIR MOST FORBIDDEN FLING	Melanie Milburne
THE LAST DOCTOR SHE SHOULD EVER DATE	Louisa George

November

NYC ANGELS: FLIRTING WITH DANGER	Tina Beckett
NYC ANGELS: TEMPTING NURSE SCARLET	Wendy S. Marcus
ONE LIFE CHANGING MOMENT	Lucy Clark
P.S. YOU'RE A DADDY!	Dianne Drake
RETURN OF THE REBEL DOCTOR	Joanna Neil
ONE BABY STEP AT A TIME	Meredith Webber

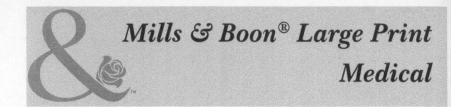

Mills & Boon® Large Print
Medical

December

January

February